L'AMOUR ISLAND

By Luna Maree

CONTENT WARNING

This book contains adult scenes – e.g.; graphic sexual scenes, and coarse language. Not all possible triggers have been mentioned. By reading further, you, as the reader, are continuing with the understanding that this book has darker tones and that not all possible triggers may have been mentioned. The author and any who contributed to this work cannot and will not be held accountable for a reader's actions, reactions, or state of mind after reading this book.

OTHER BOOKS BY ME

ALEXIS MAREE
THE KINGS OF HELL SERIES:

The Kings of Hell – Cole
The Kings of Hell - Adrik
The Kings of Hell – Malik

T. MAREE
THE LEAH REYNOLDS SERIES:

Sins in the Silence
Sins of a Daughter
Sins of the Past
Sins of the Enemy
Sins of the Forbidden
Sins of the Blood

STANDALONES

Falling for the Mountain Man

LUNA MAREE

L'Amour Island
Her Sir & Sire

CHAPTER ONE

"Sex. Orgasms. Hot, hard, *lasting* sex!" my best friend, Brianna, exclaimed.

"Bree, shh!" I scolded, looking around us at the crowded café to make sure no one overheard us.

"No! I will not. Not until you agree to take the vacation!" she continued loudly, drawing the attention of a couple waiting in line for their coffee. I gave them a pained smile before glaring back at my soon-to-be *ex*-best friend.

"I didn't even put my name in the draw to win the stupid vacation anyway; *you* did! Why don't *you* go?" I suggested, whispering loudly.

She smirked. "Because I am with a man who keeps me ridiculously sexually satisfied. I'm not the one who needs some vacation schlong."

I almost spat out the coffee I'd been sipping, and Bree laughed, handing me a napkin. "*Vacation schlong?!*" I choked.

Her grin widened, and she shrugged, unrepentant. "Yes. Melanie, you need to get some. Go get rooted, get fucked, get screwed. Go get your vacation *freak* on because honey, you are in the best damned years of your life. As your best friend, it is my solemn duty to tell you when you are being a tool. And babe? You're twenty-eight and have the nightlife of an eighty-year-old woman."

"I do not," I protested. Bree raised an eyebrow and I glowered. "I go out! I have friends; I do things. Just because I'm not dating right now doesn't mean I'm wasting my life. My life does not revolve around a man. I'm just taking some time to get over a heartbreak," I defended, spinning my cup slowly so that I wouldn't have to look at her. My chest still constricted when I thought about Warren and the two blondes I'd found him with in our bed.

"Mel, you are not nursing a broken heart anymore. A few months is nursing a broken heart; two years means you're wallowing. You were together for three years, not fifty, and Warren Pencil Dick does not deserve another goddamn moment of your time. No, enough!" she insisted, holding out a hand to stop me when I opened my mouth to defend myself.

"Bree—"

"The bastard could barely satisfy you in bed, I don't know what the hell he thought he was doing with *two* women. Except for maybe going for the Guinness World Record holder of lousiest man to have a threesome with."

A smile tugged at my lips, and I sighed. Honestly, she wasn't wrong. Less than half of the time I was able to have an orgasm with Warren, and most of those times I was concentrating *so damn hard* to make it happen, or he made getting me to orgasm seem like I was taking too long and was too difficult to make come. The other times, *I* was the reason I got off. But I hated it when Bree was right, so I refused to agree with her.

"Well, all that aside, I'm still not going."

Bree sighed exaggeratedly and dropped her head back so that she was staring at the ceiling, her inky black hair barely long enough to brush her shoulders.

"Why, God? They say you give us only what we can handle, but I need some help with this one!" she cried dramatically.

I grinned and shook my head—I loved that woman. We'd been friends for over fifteen years now, and she was always the one dragging me to parties and making sure I fully lived my life. I wasn't a downer in any sense, but I was definitely a homebody who, when left to my own devices, would take reading a book at home over clubbing and music festivals. But when I was around Bree? She had a way of making me wild, of making me fun.

Maybe she had a point; perhaps it was time I learned to live a little without her guiding me? In any case, I didn't need to start by going on a vacation that was, and I quote, *"Guaranteed to get you a vacation hook-up."*

The café door opened again, and an incredibly tall, well-muscled, *sexy* as sin man strode in. Confidence rolled off him, which, in my opinion, was half of what made him so sexy. He was wearing dark jeans and a black T-shirt that hugged his obviously well-sculpted chest and biceps. A tattoo snaked down his right arm, lending him more of a bad-boy look. His dark blue eyes stood out in contrast to his more tanned skin and black hair. He caught sight of us and flashed a half-smile that made every woman in the room stare at him with undisguised desire.

"Hello, Mel," he greeted.

"Hey, Jay," I replied, now immune to that drop-dead gorgeous smile of his… mostly.

His eyes caught on Bree, still in her overly dramatic "woe is me" position, and he smirked. I watched as he bent over her, his hand sinking into her short hair as he brought her face to his. Their lips met in a heated kiss, and I watched, part fascinated, part embarrassed—also a little wistful—as he kissed her like no one else was around. Jay once told me that the best kissing advice he had ever received came from his dad when he was a teenager.

"Every time you kiss her, do it like it's both the first time and the last time. Like you haven't seen her in months, or like you know you won't see her for a year. Do that, and she'll never look elsewhere for a kiss."
And that was what he did, every time.

And Bree? Before Jay, she was all over the place. She flitted from guy to guy, looking for something more, something hotter, something that fulfilled her in a way she couldn't properly articulate... then she met Jay at a concert. I was there the night they met, and it still made me laugh to think about it. They caught sight of each other across a crowded room. He couldn't take his eyes off her, and she kept being drawn back to him. After a few songs, they made eye contact again, and he started over towards us. She didn't move; she just watched him like she was daring him to come over. And holy hell, I had to wet my face to cool down after the look he'd given her. If a look could tell someone how hot and hard they were about to get fucked, his expression would have said it all. When he had come to a stop in front of her, they didn't even speak. She leaned up and dragged his face down to hers, and they were kissing as if their lives depended on it. She spent the night at his place, then the next day and night, and the several that followed. Finally, I officially met him, and he continued to spend all his spare time with us. That was how it had been since the beginning, and they'd been together for over two years now. My friend seemed to have finally met her match, and the same went for him if the stories his friends would tell us about him were anything to go by. He was the male Bree.

"Hi, baby," Bree greeted a little breathlessly when they finally came up for air.

"Hello, love of my life," he responded, and gave her that bone-melting smile of his.

My wistfulness kicked up several notches and I barely refrained from sighing. I glanced around to see several other women in the café looking at them as if they too were experiencing the same pangs of melancholy that I had been. I was happy for my friend, don't get me wrong. She was amazing and deserved to have a man like Jay love her so openly, affectionately, and as unashamedly as he did. But damn, I sometimes wanted to scratch her eyes out in jealousy.

"What's got you looking so frustrated?" Jay asked, taking the seat beside her.

Bree glared at me, and I raised my eyebrows. "It's all her fault," she glowered and pointed at me. Jay cocked an eyebrow in question, and I shook my head.

"Apparently me refusing to have sex with a stranger, or several strangers if she had it her way, is putting a damper on her mood," I answered.

Jay chuckled and shook his head. "The Vacation?" he guessed.

I nodded and Bree huffed. "Just… you're missing out on so much! And that wanker, Warren, doesn't deserve this much mooning and sulking! He wasn't worth your time when you were together, and definitely isn't now that you've broken up. I don't want you hiding behind your books and your job to avoid another potential heartbreak."

"That's easy for you to say. You're in love with a walking, talking lady boner. And what's more is that he's totally smitten with you too. The rest of us have to settle for the less-than-enthusiastic and try to make the best of it. I'm just not up for the drama of it," I argued, pushing my now empty mug into the center of the table.

"You say the sweetest things," Jay said with fake bashfulness. I smiled and turned back to Bree.

"Yes, I am lucky to have found Jay. And you know how I did that?" she asked. I groaned and mimicked her dramatic "woe is me" pose by slumping down in my chair and glaring up at the ceiling. "Don't think I'm done here, missy. Seriously, Melanie, I got out there. I lived every day fully and I dated men. And I knew after the first night if they were worth more of my time or not, and if not, I moved onto the next one. I wasn't shy about my hunt for a great guy, and like hell was I settling. You'll hear me make no apologies for that because it got me Jay," Bree explained.

I groaned and glanced back at her and frowned at the very serious look on her face. Bree was rarely serious; she enjoyed life too much to take much of anything seriously.

"Not all of us find our happily ever after, Bree. And not all of us find him the way you did," I reminded gently. Her expression softened slightly, and she reached across the table to take my hand, her dark eyes gentling.

"I know that, babe. But I'm too good of a friend to let you give up so early," she added. I laughed, and she smiled and squeezed my hand. "Honestly, Mel… just go on the damned trip. It's all expenses paid; it's one week of pure sunshine and hot guys. You don't *have* to hook up with anyone, although I seriously encourage you to do so. When will you ever get another chance to be someone else for a week, sleep with guys, and then go back to your life without worrying you'll run into them again? It's the perfect palate cleanser after that dickwad."

I heaved a sigh and glanced at Jay who was watching me with interest but didn't say anything. Jay was a very surprising man. He was big, bad, and tattooed. He was rough-edged and hot as sin, yet with Bree he was sweet, gentle, and honest. He kept his thoughts to himself and listened more than he spoke.

"It's only for one week, right?" I finally relented in a whisper. Bree's dark eyes widened, and then she grinned so wide she almost looked manic.

"Yes!" she screeched so loudly that she drew the attention of everyone in the café. I jumped in shock, and Jay chuckled lowly as she rounded the table and almost knocked me off my chair with the force of her hug.

"This doesn't mean I'm hooking up with anyone, though!" I reminded her as she almost choked me.

"Fine. Whatever. Let's go shopping!" Bree cried happily as she pulled away and skipped over to Jay. She planted a long, hard kiss on his lips and then jumped back over to me, pulling me to my feet.

"What the hell have I done?" I wondered aloud.

"I don't know. But I have a feeling it's going to be one of those decisions you'll forever remember," Jay answered ominously.

CHAPTER TWO

Dear Vacation Diary,

It's been a long flight.

Honestly, I didn't realize how far away this tiny island was from the mainland, and I didn't realize that I'd be seated next to one of the most nauseatingly chauvinistic and degrading men of all time. All he's done this entire time is talk about himself and rate women in their attractiveness and whether or not he'd 'bang' them. Never mind the fact barely any of the women he rated would 'bang' him even if he paid them. I tried not to judge people by their physical appearance, but when you're easily 300 pounds—almost none of its muscle—and you burp a lot and continue to eat with your mouth open while staring unashamedly at women, I think I'm safe in saying he's a pig disguised as a human male. *shudder*

If that's the sort of men I have to look forward to on this <u>stupid</u> holiday, then I'm glad I managed to sneak my Kindle with me.

Bree went through my bag an hour before I left and tossed out any books I thought to bring with me, emptied anything except for one jacket, and anything that had sleeves or material past my knees. She then filled my near-empty suitcase with clothes she'd bought for me without letting me see them.

If my nerves weren't already shot at the idea of taking this vacation alone, then having to board a plane with a bag full of mystery clothes definitely did it. And then to be seated next to a man eating, burping, and openly critiquing every female onboard the flight made me want to weep for the future of men and the women forced to settle for them.

Yep, Bitch Me is fully engaged. To hell with all men! This trip is about me sunbathing on the beach, consuming alcoholic drinks, dancing, and swimming in the ocean.

As the seatbelt light turned off, I almost lunged for my carry-on and put several people between myself and my seatmate. Thank God we had arrived!

It was only nine in the morning since the flight had been a red eye, but I didn't mind. It took almost another ten minutes to exit the plane and get my suitcase. I was only here a week, but with the number of clothes Bree had bought for me, I'd upgraded to a sizable bag rather than the small one I originally had.

I glanced around the airport and spotted a bunch of people holding signs. The instructions from the contest said that a driver would be waiting to pick me up.

Finally, I spotted a man holding a sign with my name on it. When he caught sight of me, he smiled and ambled over to me.

"Miss Gellar?" he asked.

"That's me," I answered. He was a kind-looking man. He had to be in his mid-sixties with a thick mustache I'd only known men of his era to pull off. I was getting some serious Sam Elliot vibes from this guy; only he was a little more solidly built. You know what I mean—he has the suave southern thing going for him, and despite the fact that he had more gray in his hair than actual color, you kinda find him hot.

"Let me take your suitcase. Welcome to *L'Amour Island,*" he said with a wink. "Were you excited to win the contest, miss? Hoping to find your true love?" he asked. I listened for a hint of derision or teasing, but to my surprise, he seemed utterly genuine.

"Actually, no. I didn't enter into the contest, my friend put my name down," I answered as he led me to a sleek black car. It wasn't a limo, but it was definitely fancy.

"What a kind friend you have," he exclaimed, lifting the suitcase into the car with more ease than I would have thought.

I shrugged. "She likes to remind me of this fact… a lot."

He chuckled and then opened my door. "Well, if you are not here to find love, then what are you doing here?" he asked.

I hesitated before getting into the car and sighed. "To get over being in love."

His knowing eyes warmed, and he smiled gently. "Then I think you are going to have a wonderful time here, Miss Gellar," he said softly before he closed the door.

I blew out a breath of relief at being away from the noise of the airport and steadied myself.

I hoped he was right.

~

Not long after arriving, I'd been greeted at the hotel, showered with free things, and been offered discounts across the island. Upon entering my room, I stood gaping at the sheer grandeur of the place before I did something I'd always wanted to do in a hotel room. I made a running jump and landed face down on the softest bed I'd ever been on in my life! At which point, I promptly fell asleep.

I woke up about four hours later feeling so much better about this vacation. Twenty minutes of just standing under the waterfall shower head had me more relaxed than I had been in ages. I'd brushed my hair and rummaged through my suitcase, rolling my eyes at some of the extra lingerie Bree had packed me. She really had high hopes of me getting laid on this trip. I slipped on a little light blue spaghetti strap dress and sandals, scooped up my bag, which contained my phone, Kindle, and other necessities, and had been sitting on a beach chair on the shore for the last half an hour, just staring in wonder at the different shades of blue and green of the ocean. I didn't even know water came in those colors.

I had come down here intending to sunbathe and read, but I was yet to even turn my Kindle on. The island was just stunning, and that was to say nothing of the people. I'd only ever watched movies where they had such stunning examples of the human race. I guess this is where all the beautiful people were born and lived.

Smiling stupidly to myself, I leaned back in the beach chair and sighed as I turned on my Kindle.
Perfection.

I was just raising the screen to read my newest steamy romance from Katie Rae, one of my favorite authors, when something caught my eye. It was like something out of a movie, complete with blood-pumping music and slow-motion viewing.

A God-like man emerged from the ocean, water cascading down his incredibly ripped and bare chest.

Sweet mother of lady boners.

His left arm was inked from his shoulder down to his wrist, and his right arm had a smaller tattoo on the inside near the elbow. His skin was almost golden in color. He raised his arms to push back thick, dark brown hair, his biceps tensed, and my tongue glued itself to the roof of my suddenly parched mouth. My eyes ran back down the length of him to where a uterus-quivering V led to the edge of soaking wet shorts, long, toned legs, and...well, well, well, big feet.

My face felt suddenly warm, and I was regretting not bringing down a bottle of water. I was too busy eye-fucking the image of God's gift to women that I didn't register when my name was called the first time.

"Melanie? Melanie Gellar?" I blinked and dragged my eyes from the incredible sight of his six-pack to bright, aqua-colored eyes. I blinked again when recognition flashed through me, followed by disbelief.

"Liam Mathews?" I gaped, having not realized I'd been drooling over someone I used to know. His grin sent my lady parts into a frenzy, and I forced myself to stand on unsteady legs.

"I thought that was you. What are you doing here?" he asked, that voice as smooth as ever. I always told him he should sing to more than just bar crowds with a voice like that.

"Umm...I-I... hi! I'm on vacation," I stammered, trying desperately to keep my eyes on his face as I climbed unsteadily to my feet. Well, in all honesty, it wasn't *that* hard. Liam was drop-dead gorgeous and had a way of making me feel like the only woman of interest in the room when he was around.

I inwardly sighed. Too bad he was gay.

"It's good to see you, it's been…" He trailed off almost distractedly, his aqua eyes looking me over.

It was expressions like the one he currently had on his face that had confused me when we met. I had thought he was flirting and checking me out back then, but he was one of Warren's friends, and he assured me that the man was as gay as they came. I'd been sad to hear that, but Liam had made for a good friend… whenever he'd been around, anyway. Shortly after Warren and I had gotten together, he'd been offered a job on the other side of the country and left. We saw him a few times after that, but his visits were usually short, and he'd seemed preoccupied. I hadn't even heard from him since Warren and I had split.

"Years," I finished for him. "What are you doing here?"

"I live here."

I gaped. "No way. You live in freaking paradise!"

"I know," he answered with a grin. "It's nice, ay?"

"Beautiful," I agreed and shook my head. "What have you been up to?"

"Working, really. Not a lot. Speaking of work, I have to get ready, but are you busy later?" he asked.

Butterflies took flight in my stomach, and I squashed them.

He's interested in men, Mel. As in "not for you."

"No, I'm just sort of taking it easy," I answered with an attempt at being casual.

Liam's smirk was slow, and he nodded, flicking me a small glance that had my libido revving to life. Hell, maybe he could point me in the direction of all the straight, eligible, and gorgeous men on the island. It looked like Bree was going to get her way at this stage. Bring on the sexual palette cleanse.

"Eight o'clock. Meet me at the Sandy Bar and Grill, I'll look for you. I'll buy us dinner and drinks, and you can fill me in on things," he told me.

"Okay, that would be great," I answered, my eyes running down his body again. Liam cleared his throat and yanked my gaze back to his face. He flashed me a knowing smirk that had my cheeks heating again, and he traced my face with his gaze.

"It's good to see you again, Mel," he remarked, and the way he said those words sent my heart thudding.

"You too." I stepped forward to hug him, not caring that he was still dripping wet, and he wrapped his arms around me without hesitation. Attraction sizzled, and I had to wonder if he truly was gay or if my dry spell was just causing my imagination and libido to go haywire.

Heaven.

Good god, the man could make a hug feel like heaven. He smelled like the ocean and something uniquely him. His hands stayed on my lower back and the heat of them burned through the thin material of my sundress. He turned his face inwards, and my eyes almost rolled back in my head. If I didn't know any better, I would have just thought he'd smelled my hair.

"Alright, I better go," he told me. I gave a shaky smile and nodded, stepping back. My dress was now plastered to me, and I sighed and tried to un-stick it.

"Sorry," Liam apologized with a small chuckle, but he looked anything but sorry.

"I'll dry out in no time," I waved off, shrugging. With another heart-stopping grin, Liam backed up and shook his head.

"I can't believe it's you. I'll see you tonight at eight," he reminded.

Nodding, I watched his backside without a smidgen of guilt as he jogged up the sandbank. I had about four hours until then—that was enough time to daydream and get ready.

CHAPTER THREE

I walked through the door at the Sandy Bar and Grill and took in my surroundings.

Live music played from the stage, and the atmosphere was inviting. There was a bar to the right where two bartenders worked through what I thought to be a surprisingly big crowd for eight at night. The stage was directly in front of me where a drummer, guitarist, and singer performed music the crowd was dancing to. To the right were tables and chairs, the wall lined with comfortable and intimate-looking booths.

I stepped back as a man tripped and almost went down, but he managed to catch himself on a nearby chair.

"Sorry," he shouted and disappeared into the crowd.

I peered down at the dress I was wearing, glad to see that I hadn't overdressed like I thought I did. It was a simple sheath-like dress with thin spaghetti straps, but it clung to every curve, bringing out flattering angles I wasn't aware I even had. The shoes were heels, but thankfully Bree had taken into account that I was already five foot seven, and that my balance on anything other than flats was practically non-existent. My dark hair was thankfully cooperating today, and I had tied it up in a fancy ponytail with a bit of twist. My hair apparently liked the beach life and had waved out nicely. I'd applied a little makeup but kept it light. I always forgot I was wearing it and smudged it. Besides, I was here to meet with a friend, a *gay* friend.

Tonight was about catching up, not hooking up.

I worked my way through the crowd towards the bar, deciding I'd get a drink while I waited. Liam said he'd look for me anyway.

"What's your poison?" a sexy-looking bartender asked. He was all dark and broody.

"What's good?" I'd never been a big drinker, and I stuck to what I knew. But tonight, I was feeling a little more laid back; I wanted to try something new.

He smiled and winked. "I'll look after you. Try this," he suggested. He held up a finger to tell me to wait, and I watched as he mixed a few things, shook it up, and then poured it into a glass. I waited as he added a strawberry onto the rim of the glass, and he handed it over. I took a sip and groaned at the fruity taste.

"This is amazing!" I shouted. "What's it called?"

"Depends; what's your name?" he returned with a devastating smile. My cheeks warmed again, and I grinned.

"Melanie," I answered and held out my hand. He wiped his hand on his towel and shook mine.

"Lovely to meet you, Melanie. I'm Derrick," he introduced. I smiled when he held my hand just a little too long and then pulled back. "And this drink is called Melanie's Kiss."

Ooh, this guy was good. Someone down the bar called out, and Derrick winked at me and moved along to help. I rested my hand, now damp from the condensation on the glass, on my chest to cool myself down. Holy damn, that man was hot.

"Alright everyone, we hope you're all having a good time tonight. Let's welcome on stage our local favorites, *Midnight Comet*," someone introduced on the microphone.

People clapped and cheered, and I turned in time to see Liam take the stage, guitar in hand. I froze for a second at the sight of him. He had been drool-worthy at the beach but dressed in faded jeans, and a black t-shirt that clung to every inch of him had me crossing my legs on the stool, shifting uncomfortably. Those tattoos that snaked up and down his arm only added to the bad boy look he had going. His dark hair was dry now and longer than it had been back home. The sides were a little shorter than the top, and strands of hair fell forward over his forehead as he leaned down to adjust the microphone stand. His aqua eyes were particularly visible tonight, and I watched as they scanned over the crowd. They ran over me and then back and his grin was instantaneous and sent my heart pounding.

Did he have to be so gorgeous?

"Evening, everyone," he greeted in that deep voice of his. Tingles shot south of the border. I gave up on trying to talk myself out of reacting to him. He may be gay, but he was perfect fantasy material.

"Tonight, we're going to start with an oldie, but one that has special meaning," he announced.

The crowd clapped, and I watched as he and the band started playing. The tattoos on his arm only lent to the mysterious edgy look he had, and I wondered briefly if he'd let me get an up close and personal look at them.

I was transported back to a time when I used to watch him play and dream that he was singing to me. I'd wanted him before I'd wanted Warren. Heck, I'd known Liam before I knew Warren. Liam and I had been talking for more than a week, but it had felt closer to years, and we had so much in common. He was funny and flirty and had a way of making me want to be strong, brave, and outgoing. But he also understood me in a way that meant I didn't have to explain when I needed to stay in sometimes and out of crowds and noise. He just knew.

The song sent shivers down my spine, and combined with his voice I could feel all those old feelings rush forward again. At least this time, I knew I had no chance with him.

Liam's glittering eyes found mine as he sang, and I felt my breath catch at the intensity of that stare. I could feel my body reacting to him, and all he'd done was look at me.

Shit.

I needed to get over this and hook up with a guy. I needed to do what Bree said and get me some vacation sex that would cleanse me of my past and allow me to move forward.

CHAPTER FOUR

"Thanks, everyone, for a great night! We'll be back another night," Liam said into the microphone after their sixth song, and I, along with the rest of the crowd, applauded as he and his bandmates left the stage.

I watched as they talked for a moment, several women accosting them at the base of the stairs. His bandmates were all too happy to take the attention, but I watched as Liam waved them off and headed in my direction.

He smiled and replied quickly to people as he brushed past them before his eyes landed on me, and he gave me that panty-melting smirk again.

"Hey, you."

"Hi," I answered, my voice embarrassingly breathy. Liam stepped forward and opened his arms, and before I knew it, I was enveloped in his embrace. He smelled exactly the same—warm, spicy, and a little musky—but all of it made me want to burrow closer and never leave.

"I'm glad you came," he told me as he stepped back.

I almost did, simply listening to you sing.

The thought flitted through my brain, and I brushed it off quickly and smiled a little awkwardly. "Me too. I always loved to watch you perform, to hear you sing."

Liam smiled appreciatively before he flagged down the bartender. They spoke for a moment, my drink was refilled, and I watched Liam throw back a shot of something and then wrap his long fingers around the neck of a beer bottle before turning his blue eyes back on me.

"I don't even know where to start, Mel. I guess... how's your life?" he asked. That half-smile that used to make me want to throw my underwear at him turned up the edges of his lips.

"Uh, good," I answered stupidly without even thinking. His smile just did that to me.

"Good?" he repeated, cocking an eyebrow. I watched as a strand of hair fell over his forehead, and I reached out to brush it aside before I even realized what I'd done. I froze, mortified at the personal touch. Liam seemed to freeze, too, his aqua eyes appearing somehow darker. I snatched back my hand.

"Sorry."

"Don't worry about it. You used to do that all the time," he reminded, tipping back his drink.

I watched, fascinated, as his throat bobbed when he swallowed and I licked my lips, squirming slightly. Dear God, was everything this man did sexy? I cleared my throat and quickly downed my drink, concentrating on the way the alcohol hit the back of my throat.

"Woah, you good?" Liam asked, eyeing my empty glass.

"Yep. I'm getting another," I announced and waved at the bartender. He smiled and completed his order before bringing me another.

"Want to go sit somewhere a little more private?" Liam asked. Was I fooling myself by thinking he looked and sounded hopeful?

"Private?" I parroted, momentarily distracted by my imagination. Thoughts of us ensconced in a dark corner, his hand sliding up my thigh, his lips on my neck…

"Yeah, somewhere a little quieter so we can catch up. It's been so long," Liam continued. I shook my head to get rid of the steamy images, and he frowned. "No?"

"I mean, yes. Let's go somewhere," I answered, getting up from my seat a little unsteadily.

"Are you sure you're okay?"

I laughed a little unsteadily and nodded. "Yeah, I think I downed that last drink a little too fast," I answered.

Liam considered me a moment longer before he nodded and slid his hand around to my lower back as we made our way through the crowd. His touch seemed to burn right through my dress, and I had to physically restrain myself from leaning into him and soaking in the scent of him.

Gay.

Gay.

Gay.

The man is gay.

He's an actual homosexual.

He's attracted to men. Penises. Dicks.

He is not interested in women, so cut it the fuck out!

I glowered at my responsible inner voice, the voice of reason and reality. She was such a buzzkill.

We reached a small booth in a secluded corner, and I was surprised that the music and the sound level of the patrons was somewhat muted. I could actually hear without concentrating or reading lips.

"So, where were we?" Liam asked as we slid into the booth. My lady parts celebrated when he sat closer to me so that our knees touched as we got comfortable.

"My life is good," I responded. Liam chuckled, and I smiled in response.

"I'm glad to hear it. I heard through the grapevine that you and Warren are over," he explained.

"Ah, yes. Wait, Warren didn't tell you himself?" I wondered aloud.

Liam shook his head and took another small drink. "Nah, I haven't seen him in a long time, haven't spoken to him in a little over two years."

"Wow. Glad to know it wasn't just me you've been avoiding then," I commented.

"I was never avoiding you," Liam defended quickly. I raised my eyebrows, and he rubbed the back of his neck and sighed. "Okay, maybe I was. But that was all my own bullshit; it had nothing to do with you. Sorry," he apologized. I grinned and shook my head.

"Hey, shit happens. We're here now and we can catch up," I comforted, reaching out to touch his hand consolingly. He smiled and flipped his hand over, catching my fingers in his grasp.

"True," Liam answered softly, his gaze slowly making its way back up to my face. I swallowed hard and squeezed my thighs together.

Goddamn.

"So, tell me what's new with you," I said to stop myself from embarrassing myself. Because honestly—gay or not—if the man looked at me with that smoldering look again, I was liable to lean over and kiss him.

Liam and I stayed ensconced in our booth talking for more than three hours. We laughed, we ate, we joked, we caught up on everything we'd missed in each other's lives over the past several years. He told me about his bandmates, Max, Sebastian, and Kade. He told me how he actually owned the bar we were in and that he'd bought it outright after he sold his father's condo after he'd died. The man was a brute and had never been a good father. But in his will, he'd left everything to Liam, which had given him enough to do some good in his life. We talked about Bree and Jay and how they'd met. Liam got a good laugh out of that and couldn't believe that Bree had finally met her match, a man who could handle all her fire and sass.

I managed to avoid talking about why Warren and I had broken up. It wasn't a topic I felt like discussing tonight. It felt like Liam somehow understood that, and he never pushed me for details, but that shouldn't surprise me; he'd always been good at reading me.

When the bar started to get too full of drunks, Liam said goodbye to his night manager, and we made our way along the footpath that lined the beach.

"Where are you staying while you're here?" Liam asked.

"At the resort. They gave me an incredible room with a beautiful view."

"Ah… that might be a problem," he told me, looking a little worried.

"Why?"

"Because your room is on the other side of the island. This is a small island with limited resources. We don't have taxis, and the car services stop working by eleven unless you book one beforehand. Did you book one?" he asked.

"No," I answered with a small groan.

"I'd drive you, but I've had a bit to drink tonight," he answered.

"No, don't do that," I said quickly, sighing. It had been such a wonderful night, and I'd been looking forward to crawling into that massive feather bed and sleeping late.

"Want to come back to my place?" he offered. My heart skipped a beat and my breath caught, but then I remembered that he didn't mean it *that* way.

"Do you have the room?" I asked.
He smiled, something knowing and mischievous in his eyes. "I only have one bed."

"Do you have a couch?" I pressed.

He smiled slowly and nodded. "Yes, I have a couch. But we're both adults; there's no need for either of us to sleep on the couch," he answered. I thought about that for a moment, but I was beginning to get tired, and my feet hurt.

"Okay, if that's okay with you," I answered.

"It's more than okay."

I smiled my thanks and shivered slightly when a cool breeze came in off the ocean. Liam immediately wrapped an arm around me and drew me beneath the shelter of his arm. I tensed for a second, but quickly melted against him. How did the man always manage to smell so good?

We continued our walk in comfortable silence, and when we reached his house, I sighed in delight.

"Nice, huh?" he said proudly. It was *right* on the beach. There were two large glass double doors that could slide open and gave a beautiful view of the ocean. It was a one-story, stone cottage, with wooden window and door frames, and a beautiful garden. It was stunning.

"Very nice," I agreed appreciatively.

Liam slid his arm down and twined our fingers together as he dug through his pants pockets for his keys. My heart was drumming hard in my chest, and anticipation rose. It was so stupid, but I felt like this was the beginning of something more.

"Did I tell you how beautiful you looked tonight?" Liam asked softly. I came back to myself and smiled and shook my head.

"You do… fucking stunning. And tonight was fun. It reminded me of how we used to be," he told me.

I nodded. "Me too. I missed you, Liam. We were good friends before Warren and I got together," I agreed.

"Fuck Warren for getting in the way of that," he murmured, stepping closer, tightening his hold on my hand. I was too distracted by how close he stood to really hear what he said.

"Yeah," I answered vaguely.

"I always regretted letting him do that; letting him have the chance to be with you. I stepped back, and I shouldn't have," he told me, his other hand brushing my hair back, stopping to cup my cheek gently.

My heart thudded hard, and I licked my dry lips, my body coming alive with need.

"Me too," I whispered, not having heard what he said.

"Can we have a redo, Mel? Do you think we can pretend to go back to how we were?" he asked softly, the soft rumble of his voice sending a shiver down my spine.

"How we were?" I repeated distractedly. His aqua eyes were such a perfect shade of blue, the scruff on his cheeks and chin only defined the masculine shape of his jaw. His thumb brushed over my cheek and my lower lip, his gaze narrowing in on my mouth. I watched him lick his lips and heard his swift intake of breath.

"I want tonight as a redo. To show you how we could have been—should have been—if I hadn't been such an idiot and walked away. I want to show you how we could have been if I stayed and fought for you," he replied.

"Fought for me?" I whispered, dazed. My body was in overdrive, screaming at me to kiss him, to jump him, to make him mine. I wanted him so bad I ached in a way I'd never ached before. My body and mind were at war with one another, and I tried desperately not to make a fool of myself.

Liam edged closer so that there was barely an inch between us, and I frowned when he tipped my face upward.

"What are you doing?" I asked, my heart thudding hard and my mouth going dry. I may have had some to drink, but I was definitely not drunk and nowhere near drunk enough to be misinterpreting the hunger in his eyes.

"I thought it was obvious, Mel. I'm about to kiss you. Any objections?" he whispered.

"You're not gay, are you?"

CHAPTER FIVE

Liam froze and looked down at me with wide eyes.

"Why on Earth would you think I was gay?"

"Uh… I, umm… Warren might have mentioned it before we started dating. He said he didn't want me to get hurt by letting me fall for you and then finding out the truth," I answered.

Liam stepped back and stared at me in utter shock. "Gay? *Me?*" He gaped. "That son of a bitch," he cursed and shook his head, running a hand over his face.

"So, I'm gonna take a leap and say he lied to me," I mumbled.

"That fucking ass-wipe. Warren knew I had a thing for you, so he told you I was gay so that he could have you to himself. Fucking cocksucker," he snapped angrily.

"Wait, you had a thing for me?"

Liam shot me a look that spoke volumes about his disbelief, and I grinned goofily.

"Sorry, it's just a little unbelievable and totally something I'd make up in my head; I just wanted to check," I explained.

"Unbelievable?" he repeated in disbelief. "Mel, you're a fucking wet dream. *You* are a goddamn fantasy I have not been able to erase from my mind for the past five years. When I saw you on the beach earlier today, I honestly thought I imagined it," he explained.

"Wow," I replied on a sigh.

"Gay?" Liam repeated.

I laughed lightly and shook my head, reaching for him. "If it helps, I am ridiculously attracted to you even when I thought you were gay. It just sucked more because I thought it was not even a possibility."

"You know what?" he said, and his tone was so stern I thought he was about to turn away from me in anger. "I'll show you just how *not* gay I am," he said, and before I really saw him move, he gripped my wrists and yanked me forwards. I fell against him, my hands landing against his hard chest.

Liam wrapped one arm tightly around my waist, and the other took hold of my ponytail, wrapping the length of it around his fist and pulled my head back. All of it happened so fast I barely had time to gasp before he was kissing me.

No… that's not the right word.

Devoured me, summed it up more. Liam's lips were soft and full, and yet hard and so commanding. I obeyed without thought when he tugged at my lower lip with his teeth and swept inside my mouth.

And then out the window went any kind of self-respect I had because my knees gave out, and I moaned against him. Liam's arm tightened around me, and he walked me backward until I hit the wall. He shoved a knee between my legs, and his hands slid down my sides to the edges of my dress where he slowly pulled it up.

I tore my lips from his and panted. His dark eyes were watching me with such predatory hunger, I felt my womb clench in anticipation.

"If you don't want this, Mel, you need to leave now. Because if you stay, you're not leaving anytime soon, and we're going to be fucking like we're catching up on the last five years," he warned. I swallowed hard and almost came on the spot.

Did he honestly just say that to me? Because holy fuck, I'd only ever dreamed about this, fantasized about this… I'd gotten myself off to this very fantasy.

Not bothering to answer with words, I gripped the material of Liam's shirt and yanked him back down so that I could kiss him again. A growl emanated from within his chest, and he pulled me hard against him, reaching over to open his door.

I don't remember going inside or him shutting and locking the door. I don't remember him yanking off his boots and socks or kicking off my own shoes. The next thing I knew, he yanked off his belt and stalked towards me until I backed up against a wall. The look on his face was enough to cause moisture to form between my legs. I swallowed hard as he looped the belt around a fixture on the wall above my head, his aqua eyes never once leaving my face. He took my hands and raised them above me and wrapped my fingers around the belt.

"Don't let go." His voice was so thick with arousal that I almost whimpered. Holy hell… this was beyond anything I'd dreamed of. Liam got down onto his knees and slowly pushed my dress up over my hips without looking away from me.

I drew in my first full breath as he looked away from my face and down at the tiny red thong I was wearing. It was all I could wear with this dress.

"Mmm… so naughty," he murmured as he brought his face up to the apex of my legs. His nose nuzzled my mound as his fingers slowly slid the straps down my legs. Again, I sent out a wordless thanks to Brianna and her insistence that I get a bikini wax before coming on this trip. Once I was bare for his viewing, Liam took one leg and kissed me from my calf and up the inside of my thigh before placing it over his shoulder.

Oh fuck.

His dark eyes met mine, and he smirked wickedly.

"Hold on," he warned. And then he was between my legs, his tongue sliding along my pussy and devouring me like a man starved. I threw my head back and cried out in surprise and pleasure. He made a sound that told me he enjoyed this, and I bucked my hips against his face as he gripped my hips and really went to town. He used his tongue, his lips, his fingers, and even lightly used his teeth. My eyes rolled back in my head, and before I ever would have thought possible, an orgasm slammed into me out of nowhere.

"Liam!" I cried, my thighs shaking as I rode out waves of pleasure on his tongue.

"God, you taste good," he murmured and lapped at me again. I moaned and dropped my head back, my hands beginning to ache from holding myself up.

Thankfully, Liam allowed my leg to fall from his shoulders, and I watched as he kissed his way up my stomach over my dress to my breasts. He stopped when he was standing in front of me again, his hands sliding up to my shoulders, and he helped me to step out of the dress. It fell in a pool of material at my feet, followed quickly by my bra, and his eyes dipped low to assess all of me.

"Liam?"

"Mmm?" he murmured, preoccupied.

"You're wearing too many clothes," I told him and let go of the belt to unfasten his jeans. He grinned and then took control of my lips again in a heated kiss. I moaned against him and yanked the material down. Liam kicked them off and then yanked his shirt up and over his head, and I was treated once again to the sight of a shirtless Liam. I glanced lower and groaned.

"Holy shit," I breathed.

Liam chuckled, and it sent my stomach fluttering. He kissed me again and again, and I lost track of where we were. Suddenly, I was falling and landed with a small, surprised shriek on a bed. Liam grinned and crawled over me, kissing his way back up my body, his mouth latching onto my bare breast, tugging at a taut nipple. I groaned and shifted so that he was lying better between my legs. My fingers tangled in his hair, and he nipped and suckled strongly. My hips began rocking restlessly of their own accord, and his fingers slid up my thigh to slide inside me. I gasped and ground against his hand, knowing I was just about dripping with want for him.

"Fuck, you're so wet," he murmured as if it was the hottest thing in the world.

"Liam, I need more. Now," I pleaded, desperate to feel him.

"Not yet, I'm playing," he mumbled, suckling on my other breast. I whimpered and moved restlessly against him, needing more.

"Liam," I whispered again, beyond caring that I was practically begging.

He smiled against me and reached up to his nightstand, where he pulled out a condom. He had it opened and sheathed himself in no time.

"Ready?" he asked, running the thick head of his cock against my clit.

"Yes!" I exclaimed. Liam grinned, and he watched as he slowly sank his length into me. I gave a wordless cry and panted as his cock sank deeper and stretched me.
He groaned low in his throat, and it was the sexiest thing I'd ever heard.

"Liam," I moaned, rolling my hips.

"Almost there," he panted. I watched him through heavy-lidded eyes, the concentration and strain on his face not to go too fast, the sweat beading on his forehead as he fought against his every urge to just take me. But I wanted him to lose control; I wanted him to take what I was begging him to take.

"Liam, now," I insisted, demanding all of him. All restraint was gone; Liam surged forward, sinking entirely inside me. I screamed his name, a tiny sting of pain zinging through me. I winced and forced myself to relax.

"You okay?" he whispered breathlessly. I nodded, and he grinned.

"Good. Now let's correct any notions you had about me being gay," he suggested in a low growl.

My laugh turned to a cry of pleasure as he pulled back and slammed into me.

"Fuck yes," he groaned, and I clawed at his forearms, needing to hold onto something as he fucked me harder and faster. His name was a chant on my lips. My muscles clung to him, drawing him in and milking him for all he was worth. His biceps flexed as he rocked forward, small moans spilled from his lips, and I couldn't help the sounds he forced from me. Liam pushed my legs up, and he sank deeper inside me. I could feel my orgasm building quickly. How was this even happening? I was lucky to get one orgasm a night anytime Warren and I'd had sex.

I'd never had sex like this before, never felt so full or so damn on edge.

"Come for me, Mel. I can feel you... come on my cock," Liam groaned through gritted teeth. Something about his explicit words tipped the scales, and I felt myself freefall again. I cried out as I came, clamping down on his cock hard. My breath caught in my throat, and my back arched.

"Yes, you like my dirty talk, don't you? Good girl, fucking milk me," Liam groaned, his voice almost animalistic, and I moaned and continued to rock against him, feeling small spasms shudder throughout me. Before I could get too comfortable, though, Liam pulled out.

"What are you doing?" I gasped. He grinned and slid down my body again, his mouth latching onto my pussy. I moaned and writhed at how sensitive I was.

Warren had never been into going down on me, and when he did, I could tell he didn't like it. And he never would have considered going down on my right after he'd just been inside me. Before Warren, my experience had been limited and tentative.

But Liam? It was like he couldn't get enough. This wasn't for me; it was for him. Him taking his pleasure from me, and a part of me liked him using me like this. It was so hot.

I moaned again, and he used his thumb to circle my clit over and over. I jumped and gasped when I could feel another orgasm building. Shit, again?

But before I could get there, Liam pulled away. He leaned up to kiss me, and I moaned at the taste of myself on his tongue. And then he flipped me over onto my stomach. I had never been manhandled during sex either, but this was so what I wanted. Liam was strong enough just to throw me any which way without any issues. It was scary and exhilarating.

Once I was on my hands and knees as he wanted me, I felt Liam line himself up with my opening once more. And then he slammed home. I screamed and threw my head back. Pleasure bordering on pain. I shuddered and felt him tangle my loosened ponytail in his hand, and he slammed into me again and again, riding me. I moaned loudly and rocked against him, timing my movements to his quickening thrusts.

"Fuck yes, you're so fucking tight. So fucking hot—just like I imagined," he groaned. God, if only he knew about the times I had fantasized about him. I slid my hands around my front to touch myself, only to have my hand slapped away.

"No! When we're together, I make you come. That's not for you to do," he demanded hotly against my neck. I shivered, and he bit my shoulder lightly before he licked the spot to take away the sting. He surged against me again and slid his hand around my front. He circled my clit frantically, and I moaned, feeling his thrusts get faster and harder, and I knew he was close.

"Liam, I'm almost there," I warned, almost sobbing with the need for release.

"Good girl, come on my cock again. I want to come inside your pussy at the same time. Come with me, Mel," he instructed hotly, and I felt myself spiral out of control again, reaching that impossible height with an unstoppable force.

"Fuck yes," Liam groaned, and his thrusts turned savage. His fingers never stopped playing over me, drawing out my orgasm as much as possible. I felt him shudder behind me, giving a wordless cry as he came hard.

As the last shockwave ran through me, I gasped for air and tried to hold myself up. Liam gripped me around my waist and turned us so that we were on our side on the mattress.

Neither of us spoke; the only sound in the room I could hear over my frantic heartbeat was our ragged breathing. My heart was pounding, my lungs were burning, and my throat felt raw.

"So… you're not gay." I panted.

Liam's throaty chuckle rolled through the room and grew to a full-blown laugh that had me grinning and joining in.

Holy. Fucking. Hell.

CHAPTER SIX

I woke up a few hours later, my body taught and tight with pleasure, my hips rolling of their own accord. I blinked and glanced down to see Liam between my thighs, my legs over his shoulders, my hips pinned down by his forearm as he licked and sucked at me.

I moaned at the sight as well as the feel and rocked against his face. His aqua eyes flicked up to me, and he smiled against me but never stopped. I clenched the sheets in both fists as his very talented tongue brought me closer and closer to climax. And then, as if it had been what I needed, Liam slid two thick fingers deep inside me, and my body combusted into fiery pleasure. I cried out wordlessly, my back arched and legs quivering as he thrust his fingers in and out, drawing out every last ripple of pleasure.

I sighed when he let go of my legs, and kissed his way back up my body, his hands continuously stroking over my skin, finding new places to touch. It was as if he couldn't get enough, and I was hooked on the feeling.

"Good morning," he greeted, his mouth against my chest, and I grinned.

"Are you speaking to me or my breasts?"

He shook slightly as he laughed, but he didn't raise his face.

"Both," he murmured and spent some time laving attention on them. I smiled and ran my hands through his hair. He slowly worked his way up my neck, nipping gently and sending a little shiver down my back.

"I still can't believe you're here," he whispered, his aqua eyes finally meeting mine.

"Neither can I. I almost wasn't."

"Why *are* you here?" he asked curiously. I smiled and shook my head, feeling stupid. "Oh, this will be good. Come on, you can tell me," he added with delight at my obvious discomfort.

I sighed as he laid on his side, propped up on his elbow to look down at me.

"Bree… she uh, she put my name down in a contest for a chance to win a week-long holiday here," I explained reluctantly. Liam stilled and then laughed, throwing back his head.

"You mean to tell me…" he paused, chuckling lightly. "That you're here because you won that L'Amour Island Contest? The guaranteed hook-up vacation?"

I glowered and rolled my eyes. "Yes."

Liam continued to laugh as if it were the funniest thing, and I waited patiently for him to stop. When his laughter died away, his bright eyes came back to rest on me before he frowned slightly.

"Wait, you said you almost weren't here. Why?"

"Because I wasn't interested in a hook-up. And Bree was annoying me by demanding I take a holiday and get a "sexual palette cleanse" after my breakup with Warren. She accused me of wallowing and wasting my twenties," I explained. Liam nodded slowly and traced a finger down my bare stomach, looking distracted.

"So, you haven't been with anyone since…" he trailed off, and it was then I knew for sure that he knew what had happened between Warren and me.

"Nope. Not since I walked in on him in the middle of a three-way with two stunning blondes."

There was a small silence, and Liam leaned over me, lacing his fingers with mine. I smiled up at him, loving the feel of him pressing in on me. There was something totally primal in feeling the weight of a man over you.

"Warren was the biggest fuckwit ever to cheat on you. He should have spent his days giving you orgasms and exploring every amazing inch of your body. He should have been coming up with new ways to surprise you and make you laugh and go on adventures with you," he told me, and I felt my heart turn over at the sincerity in his eyes.

"I'm sorry I believed him when he said you were gay. I had self-esteem issues he fed right into, and it explained why a man like you was even hanging around me. It would have saved us a lot of time if I'd just asked," I explained. Liam smiled softly and brushed a kiss over my lips.

"I think we've corrected that issue," he pointed out. I laughed lightly and nodded.

He considered me for a moment and tipped his head to the side as he considered me curiously. "You said you didn't want a hook-up."

I smiled and shrugged. "You will always be an exception to whatever I have planned for myself."

Liam grinned happily and leaned in to kiss me thoroughly. When we pulled apart, he stared down at me adoringly and ran his thumb across my cheekbone.

"What do you want in a relationship, Mel? Because most people nowadays simply start this way."

I considered his question and shrugged, avoiding his gaze, warming slightly in embarrassment.

"What?" he demanded, smirking knowingly.

"Nothing. It's stupid and unrealistic."

"Tell me what it is.?" He slid slightly to the right so that he wasn't crushing me, his lower body and legs still held me captive beneath him, and he kept an arm around me.

"I'm an old-school romantic," I admitted without looking at him. "I want a dozen red roses, and I want hand-written love notes. I want a man standing outside my window with a boombox playing our favorite song or climbing up my fire escape in the pouring rain to profess his love. I want the man I love to chase me through the airport just to tell me that he loves me. Like any woman, I want to be chased; I want effort and not just effort in the beginning. I want to date the love of my life for the rest of my life and not settle into a boring routine where we eventually lose our spark and forget who we are and what we mean to each other," I replied, sucking in a deep breath as I waited for him to reply.

"So, basically, you want every romantic movie from the eighties?" I laughed and nodded. "I guess so."

Liam leaned in and kissed me gently until I forgot any notion of romance and was dragged into a hazy sense of sexual need. "Let's go for a shower," I suggested suddenly.

Liam raised an eyebrow and glanced at the alarm clock. "It's three in the morning," he informed me.

I smiled playfully and shrugged. "So? I want to share a shower with you. I'll make it worth your while."

His eyes flickered with arousal, and I felt him grow heavy and thick against my thigh.

"I think we should go for a shower," he announced as if it were his idea.

I smirked and let him help me up off the bed. "What a great idea."

Liam wrapped his arms around me and walked me backward towards his bathroom, his grin contagious.

"What, dear Melanie, did you have in mind for us in this shower?" he asked playfully. My lips curved in what I hoped was a seductive smile—I loved playful Liam.

"Well, I intend for there to be lots of steam… from the heat of the water, of course," I began.

"Of course," he agreed in mock seriousness.

"And I will be wet… again, from the water."

"Hmm, interesting," Liam murmured, his heated eyes flicking down to my lips and back up. "Anything else?" he asked, and he leaned around me to turn the shower on. I waited until he'd adjusted the water to the correct temperature and his attention was on me before answering.

"Get in, and you'll find out."

Liam's aqua eyes were closer to a dark sapphire now, and everything in me shouted with joy at the heat directed at me. I waited as he slowly let me go and stepped backward into the shower. The water sprayed up and over his shoulders, water droplets sliding down his impressive chest. My eyes traced the tattoos along his left arm, down to his hand and to his cock, standing hard at attention. I stepped in after him and reached for the body soap and wash cloth. Without a word, I soaped up the material and ran it over his body. His dark eyes observed me carefully.

After I ran the cloth over every square inch of him, I washed his hair, which made him make sounds that turned me on even more. When he was relaxed and clean, I slowly sank to my knees in front of him. Liam peered down at me, his dark eyes hungry and predatory, my every move watched carefully. His glorious cock was standing at attention and waiting for me. Anticipation rose as I watched him watch me. I dragged my nails lightly across his thighs, and his jaw clenched, but he didn't move. Deciding I'd teased him enough, I slowly gripped his cock in one hand and slid it up and down the hard length, watching his face and listening to his breath hitch to see what turned him on. I flicked my tongue across the head of him, and he made a noise in the back of his throat that caused me to smile up at him. But he didn't move; he simply watched me, his dark eyes doing things to me I'd never felt before. How could this man, watching me the way he was, turn me on in a way my ex had failed to do using his hands?
I drew the head of him in my mouth, and he hissed, fisting his hands at his sides. I licked the long length of him slowly before making my way back up to his swollen head.

"Mel," he moaned throatily, almost warningly, and I moved forward, taking his hard length into my mouth as far as I could. I'd never been with anyone quite so big.

"Fuck," he moaned, and his hands came to my head, almost tentatively, as if he hadn't been able to repress that slight urge. I concentrated and drew his entire length into my mouth. I held him there for a moment and swallowed.

"Shit!" he cursed and shuddered, trying to hold back. I sucked firmly as I pulled away and looked up at him.

"Fuck my mouth, Liam," I told him. He was panting, his dark eyes blazing at me with hunger and need so raw he almost looked pained.

"Mel…" He trailed off, looking like he was holding on by a thread.

"Fuck. My. Mouth," I reiterated and drew him back into my mouth and sucked hard.

He growled, and his hips thrust forward. Elation swept through me as his hands speared through my wet hair and he tugged hard, angling me the way he wanted me, holding my head still as he thrust his cock in and out of my mouth, down my throat.

I swallowed where I could, timing my breathing to his quickening thrusts.

"Fuck, fuck, fuck," he chanted as he got closer and closer to his climax. I moaned around him, and it seemed to be the last straw.

"Fuck! Mel!" he roared, thrusting hard into my mouth, spilling his seed down my throat. I swallowed as best I could but wasn't able to get it all. He gave several shallower thrusts as he came down, and I licked and swallowed around him, my eyes locked onto his face. He was the most unbelievably gorgeous man.

He was panting now, his thighs shaky. I gave him one last suck and pulled away. His heavy-lidded eyes landed on me, and I made a show of collecting any of his cum over my chin and chest with my finger and bringing it to my mouth, licking it clean. He groaned again and tugged at me to stand up.

His hands were in my hair again as he brought me flush against him and kissed me.

This kiss was different.

He wasn't devouring me; he wasn't dominating or demanding… he was exploring. There was more to this kiss than simple sexual desire, and it made me warm from the inside out.

When we pulled away, we were both breathing a little unevenly, and Liam's blue eyes were searching mine. I didn't look away, I didn't speak. There was something heavy in his gaze, and I was hesitant to hope that it was what I thought it was.

"Did you like your shower, Liam?" I asked instead. It took a second or two, but he finally smiled. He blinked, and that heavy look was gone from his eyes, and playful Liam was back.

"I think you've proven yourself to be beyond an adequate shower partner. I'll allow this to happen again," he answered. Laughing, I backed away, but Liam tugged me forward again.

"Where did you learn to do that? Or don't I want to know?" he asked.

I chuckled and shrugged. "Bree and I were invited to a bachelorette party, and they organized to have a sex expert there. She showed us a few techniques."

Liam's eyes grew wide and then he grinned heatedly. "What else did she show you?"

I laughed and stepped away, shaking my head. "Let's get out of here."

"I didn't get to wash you."

He tugged me back under the warm spray and I didn't bother to fight it. I'd never had someone wash me before. It was one of the most erotic and intimate moments of my life, and that was saying something considering the last twelve hours, but it was. Liam was gentle, thorough—and *ohmygod*—I never knew someone washing my hair could feel *that* amazing. Liam was thorough in his washing, and he made sure to bring me to orgasm yet again, just using his hands. The man was fast proving himself to be some kind of sex god, and I wasn't going to waste a moment of our time together.

When we stepped out fifteen minutes later, we were both well-washed and thoroughly exhausted.

Liam slid into the bed beside me, and I grinned stupidly when he wrapped himself and his arms around me, hauling me close to him. I fell asleep quickly, listening to the sound of his breathing and the crashing of distant waves in the ocean.

CHAPTER SEVEN

Dear Travel Diary,

So—wow. I have no words for how amazing my night has been or how wonderful it's been to see Liam again. And wow—I mean WOW—the man is a sex god. No word of a lie. Either that or I've been settling for some mediocre, borderline boring sex over the years.

More than the sex, I forgot just how much fun Liam was. He's funny, fascinating—we never have an awkward pause in the conversation. He knows me in such an effortless way.

I've missed him.

I paused in my writing and frowned at myself. Hmm… was I getting too attached already? I shook my head and started writing again.

But, even so, all this is about is sex. Liam lives here on some kind of paradise island, and I live back on the mainland. Not to mention this was about me getting over Warren and cleansing my palate. I will not get attached to Liam. I won't let myself fall for him.

I stopped writing again as my phone rang. Closing the diary, I glanced at the balcony door where Liam had disappeared to on his phone a few minutes ago. I caught the name on my phone and grinned.

"Hey, bestie," I greeted.

"Wait, you're smiling, I can hear it. I figured you'd greet me with a few curses and complaints. But you're smiling. Did you hook up with a guy already?" she asked excitedly, and I laughed.

"This place is amazing, Bree. The island is absolutely stunning, the water is totally indescribable, and the food is to die for. It's only been a day, but I'm considering looking up rental properties."

"Well, I figured it would be beautiful. I'm glad you're enjoying yourself. You're not just reading on the beach, though, are you? I know you snuck your Kindle in your carry-on luggage. I mean, you're going to go do things, right? Talk to people, explore?" she asked.

"Actually, I haven't read a single word on my Kindle. This place is beautiful, and I was going to ask about some waterfall tours," I answered.

"I'm happy to hear it, Melanie. You really needed a break, even if you don't hook up," Bree answered. I felt my face warm. I hadn't decided whether or not I was going to tell Bree about Liam when the choice was taken out of my hands.

"Hey Mel, baby, do you want to come and meet the guys from the band? They've invited us to lunch," Liam asked, sticking his head back in the room. I froze. There was a sudden deafening silence on the other end of the phone.

"Who was that?" Bree asked softly.

"Uh..."

"*Who. Was. That?!*" Bree squealed, and I pulled the phone away from my ear.

Liam looked at me with a raised eyebrow, and I rolled my eyes and grinned. I put my phone on speakerphone as Bree continued to ramble and squeal.

"Mel, did you hook up with someone already? Ohmygod! I am so damned proud of you, damn girl!" Bree continued to shout.

"Bree?" Liam asked as he stepped into the room and closed the sliding door.

"Yup."

"Wait, did he just say my name? Why does he know my name?" Bree asked excitedly. "Wait, I don't care. Just tell me he's hot, Mel. Tell me he has a nine-inch dong and that you screwed each other's brains out last night."

Laughing, I watched Liam who looked impressed at my friend's colorful description, and I gasped as he took the phone from me and edged out of reach, grinning.

"Well, I think I am incredibly handsome if I do say so myself. I've never measured my dick but considering its size, I never felt the need, and well, a gentleman never talks about his night-time activities with a woman. However, I am not a gentleman, and Mel is a firecracker in the sack," Liam answered.

"Oh, wow," Bree breathed.

"Liam!" I shouted, feeling my face heat.

"What? She asked," he defended with a chuckle.

"Wait, did you just say *Liam*? As in Sexy-As-Sin-Gay-Liam, who you were totally considering fucking, but then Warren-Pencil-Dick told you he was gay. *That* Liam?"

I laughed, and Liam looked pleased with Warren's nickname.

"Uh… yeah. Turns out… he's not gay," I answered with a shrug and a laugh.

"*So* not gay," Liam confirmed.

Bree screamed in some kind of decibel bound to set off a few dogs, and Liam jumped back in shock.

"This is so *amazing!* I can't believe you're both there, together, at the same time. And that you *finally* hooked up! Mel, we're talking details later," Bree insisted. I glanced up at Liam, who grinned and ran a hand uncomfortably over his hair.

"Don't worry, Liam, you have *nothing* to worry about in the post-sex review," I assured.

"I wasn't worried about that," he replied with a wink and a cocky grin.

"Anyway, Bree, I gotta go. Sounds like I have a lunch to go to," I told my friend.

"*Ohmygod!* Okay, well, have fun!" she cried.

I shook my head as I ended the call and glanced back up at Liam. He was watching me with laughing eyes, and I sighed heavily and dropped back onto the bed.

"My friend is a lot to deal with sometimes." "But she got you here, so I'm grateful to her," Liam reminded, moving to lean over me.

I smiled and nodded, reaching out to trace the scruff on his face. "That's true."

Liam's blue eyes swept warmly over me for a moment before they caught on something over my shoulder. "What's this?" he asked, and I turned to see him reach for my journal.

I gasped and lunged for it, barely pushing it out of his reach. "That is… personal."

Liam looked at me with a small smirk, his eyes landing on the journal once more before coming to rest on me. "Am I in there?"

"You might be."

"Hmm… looks like I'm going to have to pull out all the stops if I want you to write nice things about me," he murmured, leaning down to brush his lips over mine. A tingle worked its way down my body, and I smiled, leaning up to kiss him.

"So far, so good," I assured. Liam kissed me slowly, intently, every ounce of his attention on the task at hand. Good god, the man could kiss. When we pulled away, I was somewhat hazy-eyed and disoriented.

"Right, we had better get going," Liam suggested. I nodded numbly and let him pull me to my feet. I quickly grabbed the journal and slid it into my small bag, looking around to make sure I'd left nothing behind.

"Hungry?" he asked as we started for the door.

"Starving."

~

I watched with an amused grin as Liam's bandmates continued to laugh obnoxiously, oblivious or unconcerned with Liam's scowl. "She—" Sebastian struggled to breathe, tears of laughter rolling down his rugged face. The guy was a Spanish heartthrob, if I ever saw one.

"She... thought—" Max tried to continue for him before he fell out of his chair. Max was a little fairer with a tan earned from hours in the sun.

"You were.... gay?!" Kade finished with a Scottish accent, his pale green eyes bright with laughter, and they all collapsed in on themselves again.

Liam sighed heavily and threw a rolled-up napkin at each of them, but his eyes were filled with humor when he looked back at me and winked. I smiled and tried not to cheer with success when his hand squeezed mine gently.

He hadn't stopped holding my hand since we left his house this morning.

"So, let me get this straight," Max interrupted, struggling to bring his laughter under control. "You were into him when you first started talking, but he never made a real move, and then

Warren came along and realized he wanted you. And so, to stop his friend getting you, he said that he was gay and then put the moves on you instead?"

I nodded, now feeling immensely stupid for believing Warren. "It was stupid on my part. Looking back, it was very obvious that Liam wasn't—*isn't*—gay. But I had low self-esteem back then, which helped me to find explanations for everything Liam ever said or did," I answered.

The guys all shook their heads and wiped away tears of laughter.

"Your ex sounds like a douche," Kade supplied.

I laughed and nodded. "That he is."

"And you're here because you won that hook-up vacation?" Max asked incredulously.

I forced an embarrassed smile and nodded. "Bree put my name down for it to get me out of the funk I'd been in. Seeing my ex, who could rarely sexually satisfy me in bed, with two women… kinda did a number on me," I admitted.

Their faces sobered slightly, and they nodded.

"And you did not know that Liam was here?" Seb asked.

I
 grinned and shook my head, turning to look at Liam, who was

watching me warmly. "Not a clue. I haven't been in contact with Liam for years."

The table fell silent as we contemplated everything that had been said, and I smiled at Liam, who brushed his thumb back and forth over my hand.

"The universe is a funny thing," Seb said softly as he raised his beer to his lips.

I smiled but realized he wasn't looking at me but the stunning redhead waiting tables. I watched as she turned and caught sight of us, but instead of blushing or smiling as I'd become used to women doing whenever they spotted this particular group of men, her vibrant green eyes narrowed on Seb, and she glowered. Lifting her chin stubbornly, she spun on her heel and marched away. I turned back to look at Seb, and the rest of the table who had gone silent.

"Excuse me," Sebastian murmured and climbed to his feet, obviously in pursuit of the red head.

"Okay, what did I miss? What was that about?" I asked.

"That was Anna," Max answered, and I waited for more of an explanation.

"Anna used to work at the bar as a waitress about four months ago. She and Seb had this flirty thing back and forth for a while, but when she told him she wasn't the kind to settle for a one-night stand, he said he wasn't interested in anything more than that," Kade continued.

"It kind of got messy, and Anna left. We all adore her still, but she and Seb can't be in the same room without fighting. I think something else happened there, but Seb won't talk," Liam explained.

"I'll say," I murmured and looked at the couple who were arguing. Anna was cornered, and Seb had a hand beside her head as they argued intently. Whatever they were talking about, it seemed messy and intense.

"So, Liam, why did you stop talking to Warren and Mel?" Kade asked, dragging us all back to the here and now. I turned to look at Liam, interested to hear this too. Liam looked decidedly uncomfortable for a moment, and his aqua eyes flew to my face as if judging whether he could answer that. He sighed and sat up straight and turned towards me.

"Warren knew I wanted you, but he turned you against me so that he could have you to himself. I'm not convinced he was actually in love with you, more that you were a prize to be won. I hung around long enough to see that you had fallen for him and that he wasn't going to run off after a few weeks," he began. I nodded, waiting.

"I really was offered a job across the country, but I was looking over there anyway. I still had feelings for you, but you were Warren's girl, and I could tell you cared a lot about him. It sucked to watch you guys, and a part of me kept wanting to punch his face in. So, I left. I thought if I put some distance between us, I'd hate Warren a little less and my feelings for you would disappear," he explained.

"Did they?" I asked softly, needing to know.

His eyes searched mine, and he finally shook his head. "No. I thought they had, but I guess they'd just—"

"Been put on hold," I finished for him.

His eyes widened, and he nodded, smiling softly. There was an intense silence as we look at one another, aware now that there was something more here than just sex. But how much more, was the question. Because feeling more than just attraction for someone didn't mean that a relationship was in the future.

Someone cleared their throat and I jumped, realizing we still had others at the table with us. Max grinned knowingly, and Kade was giving Liam a smirk. I opened my mouth to talk but was thankfully saved when Sebastian dropped back into his chair, necking what was left of his beer.

"Bloody obstinate woman," he glowered, his expression decidedly sulky. I laughed, and thankfully, everyone let the previous topic go as we asked Sebastian what happened and offered him advice. The rest of the night was spent dancing, drinking, and trying to cheer Sebastian up while the guys ribbed him mercilessly for being a love-sick fool, something he adamantly argued he was not.

I kept an eye on Anna for the rest of the night, and judging by the number of times she glanced at our group—at Sebastian—I thought it was safe to say that he was not the only one suffering.

CHAPTER EIGHT

I walked through the doors of the pub, and Liam's voice was easy to identify. I turned automatically towards the stage, and there he was at the microphone, his eyes closed for a moment as he got lost in the lyrics. The rest of his band stood behind him playing their instruments.

I slowly made my way through the crowd that was dancing to the music, brushing off a few groping hands as I did. I knew the dress I was wearing was provocative, but that was the point. The only thing was, I was only looking to provoke one man into a sexual frenzy, and he was currently singing. Not that he needed much prompting. From what I had seen, Liam simply required me to wear a low-cut shirt or cross my legs in a certain way, and he was all about getting naked and sweaty with me.

The song was coming to an end as I finally made my way to the front. The dress I was wearing was blood red and showed lots of cleavage. It hit mid-thigh, but it had passed the bend-over test in the mirror, so I wasn't too worried about flashing anyone.

Liam's eyes opened, and as if drawn magnetically, they fell straight on me. His lips quirked upward in a small smile as he continued to sing, and I felt my heart give a traitorous flutter as his blue eyes heated as they looked me over from head to toe.

I am not allowed to fall in love with Liam, I mentally whispered to myself.

A little late, don't you think? another part of me replied.

I swatted away the words, not wanting to think about the fact that, if I were totally honest with myself, I'd fallen in love with him all those years ago, and my feelings had simply been on hold until now. But now that we were together, I knew he was an option—or was he? Either way, there was no stopping how I felt.

Liam's words resonated within me as he sang the song's closing lines, never once taking his eyes from me.

As the final chords of the song faded away, I forced my eyes not to tear up. The way he was looking at me, the way he sang and watched me... God, there was no way he meant it. He was a singer. He probably used that ploy on a lot of women.

But even so...

My heart felt giddy and light at the thought of those words being meant for me.

"Thank you, everyone, for coming out to see us tonight. We'll be taking the next two days off, but be sure to come back and see us after that," Liam said.

The crowd applauded, a few people whistled, and I clapped along with them. Liam gave me another quick smile before he headed for the stairs on the side of the stage.

I watched as he barely made it to the base when he was accosted by a group of women dressed very much like me. Their smiles were full of lust and invitation. I suddenly felt cheap, like a floozy. I was not a groupie, but I had definitely dressed like one tonight. I watched as one woman flipped her shimmering gold hair over her shoulder as she laughed and ran her hand down Liam's arm. He smiled back, and I mentally shook myself. I was not allowed to get jealous; Liam and I had not had *that* talk. Besides, I was going back to my actual life in a few days. I couldn't expect him to shunt off every woman's advances. However, I was not one to share. If Liam wanted to sleep with another woman while I was here, fine, but I would not be sleeping with him if he chose that.

I considered making my way to the bar for a drink when I saw Liam remove the invasive woman's hand from his arm and gesture to Sebastian beside him, who looked only too happy to take her hand. She pouted for a moment while Liam spoke and gestured toward me. The blonde glared in my direction, and I raised an eyebrow.

Liam grinned and waved goodbye to his friends before he turned towards me. His dark blue eyes found me in an instant, and he headed straight for me, his gaze never leaving my face. There was something heady and addictive in having a man look at you like that. With single-minded purpose, with determination and want.

Liam came to a stop in front of me, and I suddenly felt nervous.

"Hey, you," he greeted warmly.

"Hi," I answered a little breathlessly. Liam tipped his head to the side slightly, his eyes questioning.

"You okay?"

I nodded and forced a smile. "Fine. You guys sounded amazing tonight," I answered, scanning my eyes over the people around us. Liam's hand came up to cup my chin, and he tilted my head back until I was looking up at him.

"What's wrong?"

"Nothing," I shook my head and pulled away.

His frown deepened. "Mel."

The way he said my name almost had me rolling my eyes. It was with the tone of someone tired of my bullshit. "Nothing, I just…." I trailed off, not wanting to admit my problem.

"Were you jealous?" he asked, raising an eyebrow, an amused smirk twisting his lips.

"No," I glared, and crossed my arms over my stomach. Liam's eyes flicked to my breasts which had pushed together over my crossed arms. I sighed and dropped my arms.

"I wasn't jealous. I just… I dressed this way tonight, hoping to keep your attention. And then I noticed the groupies are dressed the same way and… well…" I trailed off.

"What's wrong with the way you've dressed? You look fucking hot. Although you never need to worry about keeping my attention. All you need to do is to be in the same room, and you have my full focus," Liam answered. My heart tried to flutter again, but I suppressed the urge. We were trying *not* to fall in love with him.

"After seeing them and the way they all kind of just threw themselves at you, the dress just kind of made me feel… cheap," I admitted. "Even though I fully support their decision to have free, unincumbered-with-feelings-sex," I added with conviction.

"Mel... you're a fucking knockout. Everything on you and about you is real. Those women?" he began, and I started to frown.

"Don't you go bad mouthing women who like fake eyelashes and extensions and whatever else makes them feel beautiful," I warned. He raised an eyebrow at my sudden defense of the woman who wanted to sleep with him. But it was a point I was passionate about. No, she would never be my best friend, and we'd probably never hang out together given the opportunity, but I was tired of women being browbeaten by people for doing things and wearing things that made them feel beautiful and confident. I didn't care if they had hair extensions, fake nails, or eyelashes. I didn't care if they dyed their hair or wore a ton of make-up—to each their own. If doing all or any of that made her feel beautiful, then more power to her.

"I was actually commenting on her fake personality," Liam answered.

"Nice save." I scoffed. He grinned and shuffled forward, sliding a hand around my waist to pull me against him.

"There is no way in this world that you could ever come across as cheap, Mel. I know you, and I appreciate the effort with the dress... *so* much," he told me, emphasizing his point by rocking his hips against me.

A fire ignited south of the border, and I watched as he slowly brought his face closer to mine.

"Do you understand, Mel? You are perfect," Liam whispered. I nodded.

"Say it. Tell me you understand," he pressed, refusing to kiss me.

"Yes, sir, I understand," I replied, half-joking. His cock jumped against me, and I glanced up at his eyes to see them flicking with arousal. Oh… I'd found a trigger point.

"Say that again," he murmured against my lips. I smiled and swayed against him, rubbing against his hardening cock.

"What?" I asked with feigned ignorance.

"You know what," he growled, his hands gripping my backside tightly. I gasped and relished in the control I had over him with a simple word.

"Oh, you mean calling you sir?" There was a low rumble in his chest that sent off small fireworks in my lower abdomen and had my nipples hardening.

"Whatever you say… sir," I whispered, my lips brushing his. He took my mouth in a hungry kiss, and I submitted instantly.

I loved it when he went all dominant and aggressive on me. I never would have thought myself as someone who got off being commanded around in the bedroom, but with Liam it was natural, almost a need.

His fingers slid down my backside, fingertips sliding to the very edge of my dress to trace lightly against the backs of my thighs. I shuddered against him; I could feel myself throbbing and moistening between my legs. What was it about Liam that could send me into such heat with barely a few touches?

He tore his lips from mine, and we were both panting.

"This is too public," he whispered.

"Your place or mine?" I offered, ready to call it a night and spend the rest of it tied up in all kinds of positions.

"Neither is close enough—my office, now," he demanded.

"Your office?" I gaped. His blue eyes were dark and hard, and there was a demanding air to him that I couldn't deny.

"I want you now, Mel. Right now—I can't wait that long," he answered, and I was once again reminded of his hard cock throbbing against my stomach when he rocked against me.

"Lead the way, sir."

A muscle in his jaw ticked as he worked to control himself, and I was suddenly yanked through the crowd, Liam leading the way.

I caught Sebastian and Max's gaze, and they grinned knowingly. I flushed and smiled back, stumbling after Liam as he pulled us behind several dancing people, past the bar, and to the back.

Liam locked the door behind us as we stumbled inside and then quickly spun me to face him. His lips were on mine before I could adequately draw breath, the hunger in his kiss contagious. My already primed body wanted to combust at the taste of him, at the feel of his hands hauling me up against him. Breathing heavily, Liam pulled away, his heated eyes glittering down at me.

"On your knees," he whispered in a low voice. I swear my uterus started to dance at the promise of pleasure in his eyes. I hesitated a second before I sank to my knees in front of him, keeping our eyes locked.

Liam yanked his belt off. And I'm not going to lie; the hardness in his eyes was both a little frightening and totally exhilarating. I could feel how damp my panties already were and squeezed my thighs together in an effort to increase the pressure.

"Wrists together, arms up," he ordered. My breath caught, and I had the briefest moment of indecision. But this was Liam; he would never hurt me, even if he was pretending to be someone else. Besides, I was on vacation—it was time to try new things.

I swallowed hard and slowly raised my wrists towards him.

A small smirk twitched his lips, and his eyes lit with excitement that I was going to continue to play along. Liam carefully bound my wrists, and I tested my restraints. Not too tight, definitely easy enough to wiggle out of if I really wanted to, but tight enough that they wouldn't fall off accidentally. Liam tipped my head up and brought his lips close to mine.

"If I do something you don't want say strawberries," he breathed.

"Strawberries?" I wondered. That knowing glint lit his eyes again, and he grinned before kissing me deeply, his tongue sweeping inside my mouth, his lips commanding and drawing a small moan from me.

"It's the way you taste," he murmured and straightened up.

I nodded and watched as he unzipped his jeans and pulled out his hard cock. My mouth salivated as he stroked the hard length, and I swallowed. I'd never found sucking a cock to be so goddamned pleasurable in my whole life. Never once had I salivated at the thought of tasting one, but Liam? Yeah, I wanted that.

Liam's glittering eyes watched me, and my breath hitched. I squirmed again, desperate. I watched his hand stroke his hard length and felt more turned on than I could have thought possible. Why was this so hot?

"You want my cock?" he asked.

A frisson of awareness zapped from my nipples to my clit, and I nodded. His other hand shot forward to spear through my hair, where he bunched it and pulled my head back.

"I said, do you want my cock?" he repeated, his voice harder.

"Please," I whispered, unable to believe how fucking hot this was.

"Please, *what?*"

"Please, sir."

Blue eyes sharpened and darkened with lust. I could feel the dominance rolling off him, and it did nothing but make me desperate for him.

"Good girl," he murmured and angled his dick towards me. I leaned forward, and he swiped his broad head against my lips. I licked my lips, tasting his salty seed, and he clenched his jaw.

Finally, he let me take him into my mouth, and I groaned. The vibrations made him drop his head back for a moment and close his eyes, and I worked at wetting the hard length of him, all without using my hands.

"Good girl, suck my dick," he encouraged, his voice layered and breathy. His hips rocked forwards, and I relaxed my throat to take more of him. He hissed, and I could tell that he was trying to restrain himself from hurting me. But I was ready; I wanted all of him. I pulled back, and he froze.

"Please, please, sir. Fuck my mouth," I whispered breathlessly. If it were possible, Liam's cock thickened and strained even more to what had to be a painful ache.

Without waiting any further, Liam slid his cock back into my mouth and I made sure to relax my throat. He slid further back, groaning and thrusting shallowly. I timed my breathing and sucked on him hard as he pulled back. When he slid forward again, I swallowed around as much of him that would fit, and he swore.

"Fuck. That's my girl, swallow around my dick," he moaned, thrusting almost helplessly now. I squeezed my thighs together, desperate. I was almost dripping with need; I wanted it so bad.

His thrusts became jerky and shallow, and I sucked hard on him.

"Fuck!" he groaned and pulled away from me, breathing heavily. I gasped, panted, observing him intently. He gripped the base of his cock hard and staggered backward, his breathing as uneven as mine was.

"Not yet. I want to fuck that pussy," Liam explained.

"Yes, sir," I replied, watching the way arousal flickered in his blue eyes at being addressed as 'sir.'

Liam stepped out of his jeans and shoes, kicking them aside. He then pulled me up by my bound wrists and led me around his desk. He shoved a few random books and stacks of paper off the top and bent me over the wooden surface. I gasped and tried hard not to shout with glee.

"You want my cock in your pussy, don't you, baby?" he asked.

"Yes, please, fuck me," I answered, not at all playing a part.

If he wasn't inside me soon, I was going to spontaneously combust. Liam yanked my dress up over my ass, and before I knew it, there was a sharp sting across my right cheek and a loud noise. I jumped, and he spanked me again.

"Fuck, you're so hot," he groaned. He ran his finger under the thin strap of my thong and through my cheeks. I jumped and tried to edge away, but he chuckled and held me close.

"Strawberries?" he asked.

"Yes. That is strawberries," I answered quickly. Liam chuckled and continued down until he swiped a finger through my wet folds.

"Baby, you're soaked for me," he murmured in approval.

"Fuck me, Liam," I whimpered.

"Oh, I'm going to fuck you," he promised. He slid my thong to the side, and I cried out in surprise and pleasure when he thrust his cock into me. There was no warm-up with his fingers, no warning.

And I loved it.

Pain and pleasure mixed together, and he pulled back and thrust forward again, sinking fully inside me.

"So. Fucking. Tight," Liam ground out, emphasizing each word with a short thrust. I cried out and whimpered, clutching at the desk for something to hold onto.

"You're so big," I moaned, gasping as he drilled hard into me.

"You like my enormous cock, don't you, baby?"

"Yes! Harder, Liam."

He slammed so hard into me that the desk scraped forward.

There was a knock at the door, and someone tried to open it. Liam paused for a moment, and we both glanced up at it.

"Hello?" someone called on the other end. We could see the silhouette of two people—a man and a woman—on the other side. "Is anyone in there?" the man called again.

Liam began to thrust into me again, and I bit my lip.

"I swear I heard people moaning," the man uttered.

"Well, the door is locked; let's go find somewhere else," the woman answered, her tone suggestive.

Liam thrust into me harder, and I couldn't stop the small moan that escaped.

"Does that make you hot?" he whispered against my ear. "Knowing that people are just outside the door, listening to us fuck?" he asked, thrusting hard against me again. I muffled my moan with my bound hands, and Liam slammed into me harder, his hand reaching around to pull the front of my dress down so that my breasts came free.

"Does it turn you on to know that you're getting fucked while people are just feet away?" Liam asked again, his voice low and sending my body into overdrive. I loved when he used that tone. My pussy clenched around his cock, my pleasure escalated, and I teetered on the edge of an explosive orgasm.

"Liam," I whimpered, arching my back as his fingers plucked at and flicked my nipple.

"It does, doesn't it, baby? You like the idea of people getting off to the sound of you being fucked on my desk," he observed, his thrusts becoming shorter and faster.

His hand ran down my spine and then left me for a moment. And then I felt his wet thumb against my back door and stilled.

"Breathe, baby. I have a feeling you'll like this," he assured, his voice thick and breathing choppy.

Liam continued to thrust in and out of me, his pace picking up. His other hand cracked across my backside again, and I gasped, both at the sting on my cheek and the feel of his thumb sliding just a little inside my tight hole.

I groaned, the feeling surprising and invasive and yet not unpleasant.

"Good girl," he groaned, and I could tell by his jerky movements that he was close to coming. "Good girl, take my cock," he moaned.

"Please," I begged, winding tighter and tighter at the feel of his thick cock and gently thrusting thumb. "Oh God."

"Come on my cock, Mel. Fuck yes, come on my cock," he moaned, and that was it. I toppled over the edge into oblivion, crying his name. I was beyond caring who could hear or who might be nearby. The orgasm ripped through me with the force of a tsunami; my back arched as I threw my head back. Liam came hard, close on my heels. He shook and trembled behind me. The sound of him shouting my name echoed in my ears.

I stayed where I was, sprawled face down over the large desk, small tremors still rippling through me. I could barely breathe, my heart was pounding almost painfully, and I felt like a puddle of a well-pleasured woman.

"Holy fuck, Mel," Liam whispered breathlessly behind me. I grinned against the wooden desk and slowly glanced at him over my shoulder.

"Who knew you liked to be called sir so much?" I asked. He smirked and ran a hand gently over my cheek, and I clenched around him. He groaned, still gently thrusting inside me.

"Who knew you were such a dirty girl?" he returned.

"Not me," I answered honestly. Liam's dark eyes glittered mischievously, and he slowly pulled away and then froze.

A look of horror and panic took over his face, and I frowned, about to ask what was wrong when something warm and wet ran down my thigh.

"Fuck! Fuck Mel, I forgot to use a condom."

CHAPTER NINE

"Come on, baby daddy, we have waterfalls to find!" I called out early the next morning as Liam took his sweet time walking to the car. He glowered at me, and I grinned.

"Are you going to stop with that joke anytime soon? It's not funny," he glared.

I laughed and tugged on his arm to bring him flush against me. "It is funny. Your face was priceless."

"Yeah, well… I've never forgotten to use a fucking condom in my life. *Never*. But you and your hot little body and dirty talking mouth made me forget," he answered in annoyance.

I pouted and leaned up to brush a kiss across his lips. "Well, you can stop worrying. I haven't slept with anyone since Warren, and we *always* used protection. You haven't got anything catching, and I'm on birth control," I reminded him for what felt like the millionth time since last night.

"It's still not funny. That scare took years off my life! I swear, Mel, I'm never that irresponsible or caught up in the moment that I'd simply forget," he grumbled, tossing the backpack with our supplies for the day into the back of the beach buggy.

We were taking Liam's car today as some of the trails we were going to hike had rough roads leading to them.

"Liam, it's fine. I trust you. And you know I haven't been with anyone since Warren, and unlike you, I never let him forget to wear a condom," I answered honestly, flashing a grin his way. Liam fought a smile and shook his head before he joined me in the car. I think he rather liked the idea that I'd never been with a man before who had not used a condom.

"Okay, so let's get this day started. Waterfalls, coming right up. And I have the perfect spot. It's not a tourist spot, it's hidden away," he informed me. I did a little excited jig in my seat, and Liam grinned.

"You know, I've never actually seen a real waterfall," I announced.

"Seriously?" he asked incredulously, turning to look at me with shock as he pulled out onto the road. No one was up at this hour; the sun was barely climbing over the horizon.

"Nope," I shook my head. "I was country-girl born, and then I moved to the city when I was nineteen with Bree. I've been so busy working and hiding after Warren that I've never been anywhere else."

"Well, today is going to blow your mind," Liam assured me, reaching over to take my hand. I smiled up at him warmly and closed my eyes in the cool morning air that blew across my face. It was a little chilly, but I didn't care. I soaked in every moment of it, wishing I could feel this free all the time.

There was no drama here, no deadlines or stress. There were no exes, no fear, no doubts, and no crushing loneliness.

But it would come to an end soon, and I'd have to go back to my reality. The question that remained however, was I going to let life continue as it had been, or was I going to take what I'd learned here in a few days and apply it at home? Liam made me feel brave and outgoing. I could be this way at home, too, right? I could be uninhibited, unencumbered, and free of my crushing doubt, right?

Sighing, I ignored those thoughts for now and concentrated on the drive and the way it felt to be with Liam.

When we arrived at the end of the small dirt track an hour later, I had updated my travel diary and sent Bree a quick photo message of Liam and I driving. My text had been responded to with lots of heart-eye emojis, a few kissing ones, happy ones, and then an eggplant and a water splash symbol. I laughed and shook my head at my friend and pocketed my phone.

"You ready?" Liam asked, pulling out the backpack and strapping it to his back.

"Definitely," I agreed excitedly, putting on my own small backpack. Liam had insisted on carrying the majority of our things, so all I had was a water bottle, my travel journal, some sunscreen, and my phone.

"We'll keep a nice even pace. We need to walk for about an hour before we get to the waterfall, but I'll say an hour and a half because you're not used to this, and you'll probably stop to take a million photos. The walk itself is beautiful," Liam told me as we rounded the car, and he held out his hand to me.

"Okay, sounds good," I answered, not worried about the walk. Liam pulled me in close, and I smiled up at him, rising onto my toes to receive the kiss I knew was coming. It was slow, exploratory, and sweet. I sighed against him, and he smiled, his fingers gently skating across the bare skin of my lower back.

"Let's get going, gorgeous," he said. I smiled and followed him up the small hill to the beginning of the walking track. As he predicted, I made us stop at the sign and get a photo together before starting our walk.

Suffice to say, it took us two hours to get there with the number of photos I took along the way. He hadn't been kidding when he said that the walk was beautiful. Towering, ancient trees were all around, beautiful greenery and exotic looking plants, flowers, and birds were everywhere. There were moments where I thought I was going to fall down—working out at the gym in the city was nothing compared to actually walking through the rainforest with its uneven and rocky terrain and unpredictable crests and valleys. Combined with so many distractions, Liam spent most of his time making sure I didn't trip as I gaped and gasped at our surroundings.

Why had I waited so long to do something like this? One thing was for sure: I would not let myself become stagnant in the city again. Once a year, at least, I was going to plan a trip somewhere and see these amazing sights and experience things.

Bree had been right… I'd been wasting my twenties, nursing a broken heart, and refusing to get out and live life again.

Well…No more.

I could hear the waterfall before I saw it. It started out as just the distant sound of water and soon enough became an almost deafening roar. As it came into sight, I gasped and froze. I had expected to come out in front of it, seeing the massive fall of water cascade over a mountain.

I had not expected to come out almost behind it.

"Liam," I whispered, and my voice was lost amid the thunderous sound of water. Goosebumps made their way up my arms as we got closer, the water creating a cooler temperature.

"I knew you'd like it," Liam called to me. I looked back at him as he grinned, but my eyes were drawn back to the amazing beauty of the waterfall in front of me. We carefully walked closer, and Liam led me around a thin trail that led *behind* the waterfall into a cave. Seeing a waterfall from this side was something I'd never forget. Astounding, beautiful, majestic.

Liam filled me in on the name of the waterfall and the legend behind it, according to the locals. The entire time, I could barely take my eyes from it. Liam led me out the other side to a trail that led to the base. I could hear him more clearly the further down we went, and as we got to the bottom, I turned to look at it and sighed, blissfully content.

We took more photos, and then Liam led me to a grassy spot where we laid out a blanket and dropped our things.

"Want to go for a swim?" he offered. I nodded, eager to wash away the sweat from the walk and enjoy the crystal-clear water in front of us.

Dropping my bag, I tugged my T-shirt over my head and wiggled out of my board shorts. I turned to see Liam standing in the water up to his waist, but his eyes were scanning languidly over my body. I looked down and smiled. Bree had picked this out and had assured me it would drive a man mad. Judging by the look on Liam's face, it was certainly doing its job. I walked towards him and watched as his dark eyes made their way back to my face, and he smiled slowly—that favorite smile of mine that only half curved his lips.

"You really are a beautiful woman, Mel. I hope you know that," Liam said gently. I didn't suffer from low self-esteem anymore, but I knew I wasn't supermodel material. However, with the way Liam was looking at me, I certainly felt that way.

As I reached him, he snaked a hand out and wrapped it around my waist, hauling me up against his chest. I took in a sharp breath and smiled down at him as he walked us deeper into the water. I wrapped my legs around his waist and gave a gentle moan at the rigid feel of him between my legs and let him take us deeper.

With the sun shining gently down on us, Liam holding me tight, a whole oasis to ourselves, and a stunning waterfall roaring behind us, I was in heaven.

~

I snapped a photo of Liam as he lie sprawled out on the blanket, his arms flung over his face to protect it from the sun, his tanned body open for inspection. The man really was gorgeous.

We'd spent the last four hours swimming, exploring, and taking photos. We'd had sex by the waterfall, played like children, and competed for the most interesting water entrance. Liam had made an awesome lunch which we ate and then rested, and now Liam was sunbathing while I tried to capture the way the sun glistened off the water.

Little flashes of our time together flickered across my memory; the way he touched me, tasted me, the way he masterfully controlled every moment of our time together. I could feel the way it was to have him driving into me, the way his aqua eyes darkened, the way his lids became heavy, and his mouth parted as he got closer to his own climax. I swear, I could feel his fingers working between my legs, and I wiggled uncomfortably for a moment.

Putting down my phone, I walked towards him and then crouched down, slowly straddling his hips. I watched his lips twitch in a suppressed smile, and I rocked over him gently. When that didn't get a reaction, I leaned forward, my damp hair falling forward to brush his abdomen. I licked and kissed my way up his stomach to his pecks before sucking strongly on his neck, grazing over his pulse point with my teeth. He shuddered, and I felt him hardening between my legs.

I rocked against him, over and over, slowly, gently, teasing him as I locked my lips with his, my fingers raking softly over his chest. He groaned, low in his throat, and the sound sent a zing of arousal straight to my core. I was already wet; I knew I was. Being with Liam did that to me. His hands slowly slid up my bare thighs to cup my backside, where he urged me to ride him. I did as he wanted, our kiss turning passionate and heated. His tongue swept inside my mouth, and he rolled his hips beneath me. I gasped, and he pulled back, smiling triumphantly.

I quickly slid down his body and pulled off his board shorts before removing my bikini bottoms. When we were both bare, I straddled his hips again and hovered over him, sliding the head of him against me—teasing him, teasing myself.

Liam grabbed a handful of my hair and brought my face down towards his, his jaw tense and eyes dark.

"Fucking ride me, Mel," he whispered before he claimed my mouth again.

Needing no further instruction, I slowly lowered myself over his hard length and he moaned, his head falling back, eyes closed in pleasure as I took inch after inch of his cock inside my body. I slid back up and then down, taking more of him with each stroke until he was entirely inside me. My nails dug into his pecs as I rocked against him, sliding up and down his dick, every movement sending little shivers through me. I was enjoying the slow pace, building up the fire slowly and steadily.

Apparently, that wasn't enough for Liam. He gripped my hips and slammed upwards, tearing a cry of pleasure from my throat. Again and again, he did this, and I just held on for the ride. After a moment, I took control again, keeping up a fast pace.

"Fuck yes, baby. Ride my cock, Mel."

And I did.

Faster and faster, I rode, my breathing choppy and uneven, sweat beginning to glisten over our bodies as we both worked towards that incredible high.

"Good girl, ride me harder." Liam moaned as I felt myself get closer to orgasm. His hands slid up my chest to pull down the tiny triangles of my bikini top. My breasts bounced with every thrust, and he gave a deep sound of pleasure, leaning forward to draw one into his hot mouth. I gasped and rocked harder; every sharp tug from his mouth sent an answering heat to my core. "Yes, Liam," I gasped, and he changed sides.

"Come on my cock, Mel. Ride me, baby," he moaned, and I could tell from the strained chords in his neck that he was holding back. Watching the utter ecstasy across his face enhanced my own pleasure, and I found myself crying out suddenly, an orgasm sweeping through me. Liam's grip was almost bruising on my hips as he thrust upwards, once, twice, and then roared his own release.

Fuck, he was hot when he came.

I shuddered above him, feeling every small burst of his release inside me, and I continued rocking gently, riding out the small waves still coursing through me.

"Fuck, Mel," he rasped, panting. I smiled triumphantly and tried to bring my breathing back under control. "I love watching you come," I announced boldly. I'd never said something like that before. Liam's eyes opened, and he smiled, satisfied and a little cocky.

"Happy to oblige."

I slowly slid off him and collapsed beside him, and then Liam cursed.

"What?" I asked.

"What the hell are you doing to me, woman? That's now the second time I've forgotten a condom," he grouched. I laughed and shook my head. "We're protected; it's okay," I reminded.

He grumbled and dragged me closer to him, dropping a kiss on my head. "That's not the point. That is twice now that I haven't even *thought* about a condom. You short-circuit my brain."

"Is it awful that I really like that I can do that to you?"

I felt him smile against my temple, and he shook his head. "As long as I do the same thing to you."

I swallowed my smile and felt the small moment of vulnerability and seriousness that had fallen between us.

"Since the first moment we met, Liam, you've had the ability to scramble my thoughts and shor t-circuit my brain," I admitted. He hugged me tighter for a moment, and we lie in silence, both considering what this meant.

I knew that deep down if Liam wanted more from me, I'd happily try with him. But he was yet to ask, to even hint at something more long-term than this week, and I didn't want to be that needy woman. I didn't want to ruin our time together with expectations of more. I'd wanted Liam for so long and I was going to enjoy him while I had him.

~

The following two days were a blur. I'd never been happier, felt more fulfilled, or enjoyed my life more.

And wasn't that just a little sad?

Liam took me to several more waterfalls—yes, we had sex at every single one of them. One time, we were in the bushes only a few feet from tourists, and it had been both the most exciting and sensual thing I'd ever done. Unlike in his office, there were no doors or walls to prevent anyone from seeing us, just some foliage. Liam had fucked me against a tree with his hand over my mouth the entire time to keep me from making too much noise. Holy fuck… I'd never known being held down and silenced during sex could be so damned hot, but apparently, it was what got me hot and wet really fast. It hadn't taken long for me to come—twice. Once with Liam using his hand, and the other with that glorious appendage between his legs.

We had dinner once more with his friends and spent an afternoon with all of them trying to teach me to surf. It didn't go well, but it was fun watching the rest of them compete. Liam even took me to where the wild dolphins often came into the shallows, and I got to stand there while several of them swam around me. I patted a few, and Liam took photos. It was an experience I never dreamed of having, and I was absolutely speechless at having done it.

I'd called Bree once more to fill her in and sent her a few more photos. She wanted all the dirty details on Liam, but I was refusing to hand them over—not all of them, anyway. There were just some things I wanted to keep for myself. My travel diary had several more pages in it; photos, memories and things Liam had said and things we had done, but lately, they were filled with a lot of the same.

Would Liam ask me to stay? Would he ask to see me again? Did he want more than this?

Sometimes when he looked at me, it was like watching a war wage on behind his eyes. Like he wanted to speak but was holding himself back. Maybe it was just wishful thinking on my part, but he had a tendency to get serious sometimes, and I desperately wanted to know what he was thinking.

We'd enjoyed our time together, but now Liam had a life to get back to, and so he would be working late for the next few nights. He and his band perform most nights, but he also has to keep up with the books, orders, staff, and managing the business itself. I would spend the days with him though—he insisted—and then I could do what I pleased. But really? I didn't want to be anywhere else but with him. Desperate and pathetic, I know. But my time with Liam was running out, and even if I could only watch him while he worked, it felt like it was all I was going to get, and so I took the opportunity with two hands.

Our time together had been so magical, I just didn't want to give it up.

CHAPTER TEN

Liam had taken me back to his house after we spent the following day clothes and souvenir shopping and doing a little grocery shopping for his kitchen. We'd had incredible, hard sex twice, and then he'd left me asleep in bed while he went to work. I woke to find a flower and a note on his pillow telling me he couldn't wait to see me again and that I was welcome to stay and make myself at home while he was at work.

I'll admit, I wanted to stay and sleep, but I wanted Liam more. Having woken up without him beside me had been an eye-opener, though. I was definitely way too attached to the man because I hated waking up and not seeing him there. The note was sweet, as was the flower, but it had given me a brief glimpse into how my life was probably going to be without him in it, and I didn't like it at all. "Hey babe, how's the sex? I mean, *the holiday?*" Bree greeted when I called her.

I threw myself back into the soft mattress and sighed. "Uh-oh, that doesn't sound good. What's wrong?" Bree continued.

"I think I'm in trouble, Bree," I admitted.

"What kind of trouble? Do I need to bring bail money? A shovel and some lime? Or a therapist?"

I gave a small laugh and shook my head, mostly because I knew she would be down for any option, she just wanted to know what to expect. There was a reason she was my best friend.

"None—maybe the therapist, we'll see. But... I think I'm way in over my head here." My voice was quiet when I responded, and the sadness on my heart was beginning to weigh too much.

Bree was silent for a moment, and then I heard her sigh. "You're in love with him."

"No," I denied immediately. "No, I mean—we've only been seeing each other for a few days, and we both know it's temporary."

"You may have only been seeing each other for a few days this time, but it's been an intense few days. And let's not forget that you two met a long time ago and hit it off like you were meant to be. I never knew two people could connect so quickly," she told me. I scoffed.

"Says the woman who spent an hour eye-fucking a man, then kissing him without so much as a "hi, my name is Bree." You've been with the guy for ages, and you two are so in sync it's almost sickening," I reminded.

She gave a small laugh, and I could picture her shaking her head and rolling her eyes.

"Okay, so Jay and I are the exceptions. But seriously, Mel. You two had something back then. You had a lot of chemistry and… well… you're different with him. Even speaking to you over the last few days, I can hear that he still makes you different. He makes you confident and calm. He makes you happy. And that's how you two were five years ago. So, it's not crazy if you *are* in love with him now," she explained.

I ran my hand over my face and shook my head, not wanting to entertain the thought.

"Love, lust… whatever this is… it's dangerous. I'm leaving soon. I have two more nights here and tomorrow is pretty much my last day since I leave the following morning. And I just… if he wanted more from me, he'd tell me, right?" I asked.

"Hon, you really need to be talking to him about this. Usually, I'd say yes, but…"

"But what?" I pushed when she trailed off.

"He knows you were there because you won the hook-up vacation. Maybe he thinks this is all *you're* after?" she suggested. I frowned; I hadn't thought of that.

"And if he's not?" I asked, my voice barely above a whisper. "What if I am falling for him and he wants nothing more… What do I do then, Bree?" I asked, my eyes stinging at the thought and my chest aching.

Bree was silent for a moment, and then she sighed heavily.

"Then, baby girl, you get on that plane and come home. I'll be here waiting, and we'll get you through this, but you will not leave that island with a single regret. You needed this. You needed to meet him again and remember who the real you is," she answered. A tear escaped from my eyes, and I brushed it away quickly and cleared my throat. It was a lot easier said than done, but she was right. What other option was there?

"Are you okay?" she asked softly.

"I'll be fine. I just… I woke up alone in the bed for the first time since we reconnected. It just gave me a bit of a reality check."

"Don't get down on yourself now, okay, Mel? You have some time left on that island, enjoy every moment, and enjoy that sexy man who is more than happy to be with you," she encouraged, inserting pep and excitement into her voice.

I laughed because I knew she wanted me to and dragged myself into a sitting position. My hair fell forward over my shoulders, and I grimaced at the knots. Maybe it *was* better that I woke up alone this evening.

"Alright. Liam is singing tonight, so I'm going to go to the bar to see him. I'll talk to you again before I leave. Thanks, Bree," I told her.

"No worries, babe, that's what I'm here for. Enjoy," she called. I smiled and hung up, sighing heavily. She was right. I could not and would not ruin the rest of my time here by being depressed and upset, worrying about the future.

The present was here, and it was outstanding.

~

When I arrived at the pub an hour later, everything was in full swing. I knew Liam had needed to go in early to deal with some paperwork for the bar. He'd spent so much time with me over the last few days that he'd fallen behind, and he'd already admitted to hating the paperwork side of things and letting things slide longer than he should.

I entered the Sandy Bar & Grill and almost immediately felt Liam. My gaze swung to the stage, and there he was, singing into the microphone, his burning blue gaze on me. I smiled, my heart fluttered, and my stomach flipped. He grinned, and I couldn't stop the wave of heat that washed over me at that look.

How was it he always seemed to know where I was in a room? Was he looking for me, or did he feel this crazy magnetic pull between us as well?

I waved up at him, and he waved back, never once missing a beat. I made it to the bar, and Derrick was working again.

"Hello to the woman who broke my heart. I should have known you'd fall for the lead singer," he greeted. I smiled back, happy that he hadn't taken our small flirt the other night seriously.

"I'm very certain that it was not your heart I broke. I might have bruised your ego though," I replied. He grinned and shrugged. He really was a stunning man.

"Would you care for your signature drink?" he asked. I nodded, and he got to work. I glanced around the room at all the people dancing, swaying, laughing, and having an overall good time.

I'd worn another dress this time, black, and it had spaghetti straps that crisscrossed up the back. A part of me had gotten excited, envisioning us using Liam's desk again. A shiver ran up my spine at the thought of it, and I smiled my thanks at Derrick as I paid for my drink, and he placed it on the bench in front of me. I turned to the stage to see Liam open his eyes, and his gaze clashed with mine. I smiled, wishing I didn't feel my heart leap at that smile.

Bree was right. If I was honest with myself... I'd fallen for Liam years ago, and instead of the feelings dying off when he left, it was like we had put them on hold until we saw each other again. Now that we were here, together, they were raging back at full force.

And he still hasn't asked me for more.

I brushed away the thought and reminded myself that I hadn't exactly been upfront with him about my feelings, either. Liam was a man who went for what he wanted. If he wanted more with me, he would have said so. But no matter what, I wanted to look back at my time on this island with fond memories. I didn't want to ruin all of this by pushing for more than he was willing to give.

Liam and the band finished playing, and I clapped along with the crowd. Finishing my drink and waving goodbye to Derrick, I made my way over to the stage where Liam was looking for me. Seb and Max waved, and Kade grinned at me.

"Hey, you," Liam greeted and kissed me soundly. I smiled, and he brushed a thumb over my cheek. "I just have some things to sort out with the boys backstage, then I'll come and find you," he told me.

"Sounds good," I answered, kissing him quickly before he and the guys headed off. I made my way into the dancing crowd. The music was playing through the sound system, and I loved the beat.

I closed my eyes and let myself get lost in the music, swaying and rocking along, having a good time with everyone else in the crowd. As the tempo picked up, I was right there with everyone, jumping up and down and cheering.

A pair of large hands slid around my waist, and I leaned back into him, rocking my hips from side to side. It only took me a couple of seconds to realize it wasn't Liam. I spun and stepped away immediately, and the tall man smiled encouragingly back at me.

"Sorry, I thought you were someone else," I explained, having to shout to be heard over the music.

"I can be whoever you want me to be," he answered. I rolled my eyes at the comment but couldn't help smiling when he grinned. "Thanks, but no thanks," I replied politely. I moved away a little and continued to dance, determined to enjoy myself. A body pressed against me again, and I looked over my shoulder to see the same man.

"No," I said firmly, turning to look at him.

"Oh, come on. You can't wear a dress like that and dance the way you were, and expect a guy to stay away," he joked.

At once, I felt the age-old weight that all women have worn over the years press down on my shoulders. I wanted to scream in frustration and castrate the man in front of me in one move.

"And yet you talk like that and wear that face and expect *not* to get punched in the face. I guess we all expect to be treated like human beings and not objects."

He scoffed.

"Right, I should have known that you were one of them. Those feminist bitches who like to tease a guy but never put out."

I wanted to take a step back from the sheer acid dripping from his tone, but I didn't. I forced myself to hold my ground.

"And those are the words of a man with a bruised ego, tired of being turned down by women who get a sense of the kind of asshole you are and decide they can do better."

"Typical. Such a fucking tease. You dress like a slut, and the second a guy puts his hand on you, you can't wait to tell him he's overstepping and you're too good for him," he argued, venom laced in every word. This was one ugly and very bitter man. People around us were noticing, but I wasn't worried about creating a scene.

"I've said no. You can leave now," I answered.

"Or what?" he sneered and stepped closer, gripping me by the hips and hauling me up against him. I struggled for a moment, and he moved his hands to my upper arms and pulled me closer, bending his head towards mine. As tightly as I was pressed against him, I felt his cock hardening in his pants and felt sick.

"Fuck off."

"Screw you, you uppity bitch," he hissed and tried to kiss me. I threw my head forward and smacked him hard in the lip. His head snapped back, and I ignored the pain in my forehead as he loosened his hold on me. I wrenched myself free and was about to kick him where it would hurt the most when someone launched themselves at him.

"Liam!" I shouted as he laid into the guy, punch after punch to his face.

"Stay. The. Fuck. Away. From. Her," Liam snarled, punctuating each word with a punch.

"Liam, stop!" I shouted, trying to pull him off the guy. I didn't give a shit if the guy needed plastic surgery after this; I just didn't want Liam to get into trouble.

A few other guys pulled Liam off the asshole and stepped in between them. Liam tried to lunge back at him, but the guys stopped him.

"She said no, fuckwit!"

"Fuck you!" the guy shouted back, but his voice sounded thick and pained.

"Get the fuck out of my bar!" Liam ordered.

At this point, the music had stopped, and everyone was watching the scene before them. A guy helped the douchebag to his feet, and they stumbled out of the bar. The asshole snapped and snarled the whole way, but he walked away under his own steam.

"Okay, everyone, wasn't that exciting?" I turned hollowly towards the stage to see Sebastian up there, trying to draw attention away again. "We take women's safety seriously here, so let's make sure everyone is a willing partner tonight, eh? Alright, let's crank this music back up and have some fun!" Seb shouted and turned the music back on. Everyone cheered and started dancing again as if nothing had happened, but I was watching

Liam, who stood there, his chest heaving and his face murderous. "Liam, what the hell?" I was panicked that he'd done something he'd get into trouble for later.

He glowered at the doorway where the man had disappeared and then turned to look at me. "He had his hands all over you."

"And I was dealing with it. I would have handled it until you came in and went all possessive alpha-male."

"Liam," Max interrupted, weaving his way through the crowd. "I just spoke to some witnesses, they all say they heard her say no several times, and he wouldn't back off. They're giving their statements now to Seb that you were defending her. I don't think there will be any trouble here," he explained. My shoulders sagged in relief, and I smiled thinly at Sebastian as he nodded at me and disappeared. I turned back to Liam, who was still looking furious.

"He shouldn't have been touching you, Mel," he growled.

"Yes, I know that," I replied, my tone conveying the obviousness of his statement.

"You're not his to touch. No one else."

No one else's... just his?

I shook my head at the thought. I wasn't a toy to be fought over, not even for Liam. I appreciated him coming to my rescue, but if he'd given me another moment, I would have handled it myself.

"Liam, I told him to go away; I'm not an object to be handled. Not by him, you, or anyone," I reminded.

"I know."

"So then, what the hell was that?" I repeated, gesturing towards the door the asshole had left through.

His blue eyes met my gaze, and he glowered. "He just… he shouldn't be touching you, okay?"

I frowned at how angry he was and then gasped when he suddenly gripped my wrist and pulled me towards the front door.

"Liam," I called, frowning as he pulled me outside. He tugged me down the steps and down the small alleyway between the bar and the building next door. No one was looking in our direction, and thankfully there was no sign of that asshole or any cops.

"Liam, what are you doing?" I demanded in a hushed tone, looking over my shoulder, but no one was looking at us; no one followed. He kept tugging me down the alley until we reached the end and were shrouded in shadows. Then he swung me around until I was backed against the cold stone wall. I looked up to demand an answer, but his lips came crashing down on mine. Hard, hot, possessive. I tried like hell not to react to his kiss—I was angry, dammit!—but it was impossible. I moaned, and his hands began tugging up my dress, his knee shoved between my thighs. I gasped, and he used his hands on my hips to help me ride his thigh, his tongue mating with mine in a kiss so scorching hot—I was amazed our clothes didn't catch fire. This wasn't to make his point; this was a branding, a claim. He was saying that he owned me, and if he was saying that, then I would claim him right back.

I slid my hands down to his belt and quickly unbuckled it, uncaring that we were supposed to be fighting right now. His hands slid to the edges of my underwear, and he growled and tore them clean from my body. I yelped in surprise, liquid heat pooling low.

Shivers of pleasure ran down my spine, and I panted as he nipped at my neck, and I opened the top of his jeans. Liam let go of me long enough to shove them down and pull out his cock, already erect and swollen.

"Liam," I breathed, almost begging.

"Hold on to me," he whispered, his voice low and gravelly. I gripped his shoulders as he lifted me up and pinned me against the wall before he lowered me over the hard, throbbing head of his cock. His name came out like a whimper, and he hissed.

"Fuck, you're always so wet and tight," he growled and thrust hard into me. Pain and pleasure mixed, and I cried out, not caring right now that my voice echoed in the small alley.

"You're mine, Mel. Mine," he growled and began thrusting into me, hard and fast. I held on for dear life, my nails digging into his shoulders, and my head was thrown back. "No one touches you," he panted, his hips snapping hard against me. "You're mine, Mel. Say it."

His blue eyes alight with a kind of passion and savagery I had not seen in him before. What was so wrong with me that all it did was turn me on even more? I teetered on the edge of orgasm, but Liam stopped moving, refusing me my pleasure.

"Mine. Say it, Mel. Tell me you're mine," he whispered unsteadily, holding my head back so that it forced me to look into his eyes.

"I'm yours, Liam. Just yours." As the words left my lips, I couldn't help feeling as though I'd just agreed to something totally irrevocable.

Liam kissed me hard again, slamming into me repeatedly and I cried out, feeling myself shatter around him; stars burst behind my eyes, and my throat felt raw. Liam was right there with me, coming so hard that he shuddered, his wordless cry echoing my own. He continued thrusting in and out of me in small, quick thrusts for a moment before we both dragged in a deep breath.

Slowly, he put me back down on shaky legs, and I held onto him for a moment before I pulled my dress back down, and he tucked himself away again. I reached up to cup his face, and it took him a moment to meet my gaze. I had questions, but right now, I knew it wasn't the time to get them. He looked mad, vulnerable—almost scared and pained.

Instead of asking him what he'd meant or what all that had been about, I leaned up and brushed my lips gently over his.
"Let's go."

Liam nodded slowly and dragged me to him, wrapping me in his strong embrace for a moment. Neither of us spoke, but we both seemed to be soaking in as much strength from the other as possible.

Was he feeling as helpless as I was about this whole situation?

He reluctantly let go, but he never relinquished my hand. We made our way back to Liam's house in silence, slowly, neither of us knowing what to say now. All I knew was that I was going to be replaying that moment in my head for a while longer, until it all made sense.

You're mine, Mel. Mine.

I'm yours, Liam, just yours.

Chapter ELEVEN

That night we walked home in silence. Once we reached his house, Liam pulled me straight into the bathroom where he took his time undressing me, brushing his lips over every available inch of my body. It was almost like worship, and it made me feel so treasured. After he'd kissed every part of me that he could, I forced him to stand. I undressed him, and when he was naked, I took his hand in mine and looked down at his knuckles. They were slightly bloody and a little swollen. We showered in silence. He ran the cloth and his hands over me several times, taking special care to wash my hair. He brushed his thumb over my forehead, and I winced. I was probably going to have a bruise on my head. He kissed it and continued to wash me. And then it was his turn. He stood there in silence, his dark eyes watching my every move as I ran my hands over every inch of him; cleaning him, touching him, memorizing the feel of his body, engraving him into my mind.

Without either of us saying a word, he slid inside me. It was so different compared to every other time we'd been together. It was slow, intense, and deep; neither of us spoke. There was no pleading, no begging, no teasing, or dirty talk. And somehow, it was so much more than every other time we'd been together. The surrounding air was heavy with words unspoken and unasked questions, but neither of us seemed ready to go there. He wasn't avoiding me, nor was I avoiding him.

We couldn't seem to keep our hands to ourselves. I'd never had a night like it. We were both so lost, and I wondered for the millionth time—*was* I his? Did he really want me to be his, or was he just marking his territory while other men were around?

~

When we woke in the morning, it was as if the previous night had never happened. The air was no longer weighted and thick. Liam woke up smiling and kissed me good morning, and then after making sure I was thoroughly ready for him, he was inside me in no time. We continued with what seemed to be our morning ritual since I'd been here. We always woke up and devoured one another in some form or another, starting the day by sharing my body.

Liam flipped us over so that I was on top, and instead of letting me ride his cock, he urged me further up his body. Insecurity and awkwardness tried to take over, but one look at his eager face had me going for it. I straddled his shoulders, and Liam hooked his arms around my waist and brought his mouth to my pussy. I moaned as he buried his face hard between my thighs, and I rocked against his mouth, my head thrown back and eyes closed. I gripped the headboard tightly as Liam devoured me.

It was a different experience, but this way allowed for his tongue to slip inside me so much further than before.

"Liam, yes," I panted, rocking faster against his mouth. He slid a finger deep inside me, followed by another, giving me something hard to ride.

I groaned and rode them harder. And then his fingers slid around my back, and he massaged my back door. I stilled and looked down. His aqua eyes watched me intently, questioningly, eagerly, as he slowly teased a finger inside me. I moaned at the sensation, closing my eyes at the near taboo feeling of it all. He continued to lap at me, sucking hard as he slowly pushed his finger in and out of my other hole. I rocked against him, not hating the feeling but not sure if I loved it yet or not either. When he started to insert a second finger, I shook my head, straining my memory for that word.

"Strawberries," I gasped, and Liam smiled against me, removing the second finger. I wasn't ready for that; I wasn't sure I'd ever be ready for that. But so far, one finger was more than enough. Liam adjusted his hold on me, and I was moaning his name again, overwhelmed by the sensations flooding me as he licked my pussy and continued to thrust a finger in and out of my back door.

"Liam," I chanted, getting closer and closer to the edge. He doubled down on his efforts, and I moaned again, shattering, coming hard. I barely hit my pleasure when Liam slid out from under me and gripped my hips. Still gripping the headboard, I had time enough to brace before Liam slammed into me from behind.

I threw my head back and called his name, feeling him fill me completely. My inner muscles were still rippling from my orgasm and felt another follow quickly on its heels as Liam continued to thrust into me with his cock, over and over again, his thumb back in my back door.

I knew it was dirty, knew I probably shouldn't like it as much as I did. But goddam, I loved it when he pushed my limits.

His grip on my hips tightened, his thrusts turned shorter and rougher.

"Come inside me, Liam," I gasped. "Fuck me harder."

Liam swore and picked up the pace, slamming into me so hard that the headboard hit the wall. I gripped the headboard until my knuckles turned white, bracing, and pushing back against him as he gave me his all.

"Fuck, fuck, Mel, fucking yes!" Liam shouted loudly before I felt him shake and shudder behind me, shooting deep within me. I struggled to draw in a breath and could still feel myself rippling around him. I clenched my inner muscles, and he groaned and shuddered again.

"God, stop—too sensitive," he moaned. I clenched again, and he shook hard and groaned. I smiled and waited as he slowly slid from me, wrapped an arm around my waist, and pulled me down next to him. His breath was hot and uneven against my neck, and I could feel his heart slamming hard in his chest as it pounded against my back. I was glad to see we were well past him worrying about forgetting to wear a condom.

"Good morning," I greeted. Liam shook gently as he laughed, and he kissed my bare shoulder. "Good morning, baby."

My smile slowly faded as I remembered what today was. This was my last day. I had one more night and one more day here with Liam, and tomorrow morning my flight would leave at six a.m.

Slowly, it was as if Liam remembered too, and I could feel the melancholy press down on us. Liam's arms slowly tightened around me as if he were afraid I'd disappear from his arms. I didn't move, quite happy to be here all day.

But of course, that wasn't going to happen.

Liam's phone rang on the bedside table, and he sighed heavily before he kissed my head and grabbed it. Before I could roll away, however, he rolled back over, keeping me pinned to him as he answered.

"What's up, Seb?" he asked.

"Are you panting? Did I just catch you after sex?" I heard Sebastian ask. My face warmed as I hid my face against Liam's chest, and he laughed.

"Yes. Now what do you want?" Liam said without a qualm.

"Fucking lucky bastard," Sebastian swore. "I spoke to Morrison down at the station this morning. That fucker from last night tried to press charges against you, but with our witness statements, Morrison threatened to charge the shithead with attempted sexual assault, and he dropped it quick. I've informed him he has a lifetime ban from the bar and that we're sharing his face around to the other bars. He'll be lucky to get a drink on this island ever again," he filled in.

"Thanks for handling all that, Seb," Liam replied solemnly.

"Yeah, yeah. So, do we get to see the lovely Mel today before she has to leave? Or can we expect you two to be locked inside your house all day?" Sebastian asked.

"What do you think, Mel?" Liam asked. I grinned up at him and sighed heavily, knowing Sebastian could hear me.

"I'd love to stay in bed all day, but you're insatiable. I'd like the ability to walk tomorrow," I answered as if it were such a burden. Liam chuckled, and Sebastian swore again.

"We'll meet you guys for an early dinner tonight. What do you think?" Liam asked.

"Sounds good; I'll let the guys know," he replied. Liam said goodbye and hung up. As he brought his arm back around, he spun me onto my back so that he was leaning over me, and I smiled up at him.

"Waking up to you in my bed, in my arms, has been the best feeling in the world," Liam told me seriously. I smiled, and my heart fluttered again.

"Waking up here has been the best feeling," I replied. His smile was soft and slow, and he gently brushed my hair back, his eyes turning dark as he gently traced a finger around the spot on my head where I'd hit that douchebag.

"I'm sorry you saw me lose my temper," he murmured regretfully.

"I was worried you were going to get into some serious trouble, Liam," I explained. He nodded slowly and gently brushed back my hair.

"I don't regret it, though. Men like him need to understand that sort of behavior is not okay. And I'm not about to sit by and let it happen. If he won't listen to a woman when she says no, he'll fucking listen to a man when his fists hit his face," he told me, his voice seeming to dip lower when he got angry.

"Hey," I whispered, bringing my hands up to cup his face. "It's done now. Let's not let it ruin the day."

Liam nodded, slowly dipping his head to kiss me. The kiss went on and on, soft and deep, languid and exploratory. So much went with that kiss that I just sunk into it and enjoyed it while it lasted.

~

The day seemed to fly by, and I hated it. I was scrambling to soak in every moment, document it, take photos, and enjoy it all. But there weren't enough hours in the day. Liam seemed to be constantly touching me, holding my hand, wrapping his arms around me. We were barely apart.

Then, before I was ready for it, I was dressing, getting ready for dinner with the guys. I was wearing a simple dark blue halter neck shirt and a swishy black skirt. The shirt was mostly backless, so I wasn't able to wear a bra. I had the perfect little black strappy shoes to go with the skirt. All I needed was to do my hair, and I was ready. Liam stepped up behind me in the full-length mirror and wrapped his arms around me. I smiled and leaned back into him.

"You look beautiful," he whispered against my ear, sending goosebumps down my arm.

"You look rather handsome yourself," I replied, taking in his worn-looking blue jeans and the black button-up shirt he was wearing. His eyes glinted back at me in the reflection, and I swallowed at that look. I knew that look very well. His hand slid up my stomach to cup my breasts, and he pressed himself harder against me, groaning when he realized I wasn't wearing a bra.

"No bra?" he murmured.

"I can't with this shirt," I replied, rolling my neck and arching my back.

"Very naughty," he said in a low, growling voice, nipping at my earlobe. A sort of throbbing started down low, and I pressed my thighs together to increase the pressure where I needed it. I *loved* that voice.

My nipples hardened and pebbled beneath his hands as he brushed his fingers over them through my shirt. "And are you wearing underwear?" he asked softly, slowly sliding his hands down to my front.

"Liam, we have to get going," I reminded only half-heartedly. "Mm-hmm," he hummed, slowly tracking his hands back up my thighs. I watched with bated breath as he bunched up my skirt, revealing inch after inch of bare thigh.

"Liam," I breathed, my heart pounding in anticipation, my body primed and ready.

"A little black thong," he noted, hooking his thumbs in the sides as he dragged the thin scrap of material down. I opened my mouth to protest, to remind him we had plans, but his teeth were making little nips down my neck, and I moaned instead, kicking the material away from me as it slid down my legs.

"Are you wet for me, Mel?" he whispered darkly.

"Y-yes," I stammered, my tongue seeming to not want to work.

"Tell me," he demanded, biting a little harder on my neck. My knees actually shook, and I arched my back, trying to get him to touch me where I wanted him most.

"Tell me, Mel," he urged.

"I'm wet for you, Liam," I answered in a rush. He slid his hand further under my skirt, and I bit my lip when he slid a finger through my wetness to circle my clit.

"Mm, baby. I'm going to make you come," he decided.

"Liam... we have... plans." I tried one more time, all the while pressing myself into his palm.

"They can wait," he answered and slid two fingers deep inside me. I cried out and bucked against him, and Liam reached around with his other hand to untie my halter top and let it fall down my chest, exposing my breasts.

"Fuck," he groaned and palmed one, his thumb and forefinger rolling the hard nub while his fingers on his other hand thrust in and out of me.

"Liam, I'm going to come," I panted.

"Not yet, baby," he said and pushed me down onto my hands and knees. He quickly unbuckled his belt and shoved down his pants before he positioned himself behind me. I waited, and he wrapped a hand around my hair and pulled my head back, and I found myself staring at us in the mirror. "Who do you belong to?" he asked, and I shivered at the dark demand in his voice, the need. Never in a million years would I have thought having a man order me to admit that I belonged to him to be sexy, to be so damned hot. But holy fuck. I was well and truly his.

"Yours," I answered without hesitation. And then Liam slammed inside me. I cried out, my back arching as he filled me. Once again, I balanced on that edge of pleasure and pain that I had quickly become addicted to and barely had time to drag in a breath before he pulled back and thrust inside me again.

"Watch, Mel. Watch me claim you. You're mine, baby," he groaned and thrust into me, over and over.

"Mine," Liam gritted out and moaned.

"Yes," I whispered jerkily. So damned... close. I could feel his thick cock inside me, sliding in and out as he thrust harder and harder. His face was contorted in lines of concentration and pleasure. His hand slid around my front, and he flicked at my clit, rubbing it in small, quick circles until I could feel my orgasm building towards an impossible height.

"Liam," I pleaded.

"Come on my cock, Mel. Come for me, baby," he ordered. As if that was all I needed, I climaxed. I shattered around him, hitting that pinnacle with a dizzying speed. I screamed his name, my body shaking and quivering around him, clamping down hard on his cock. Liam cried out, my name tumbling from his lips. His neck was corded with veins and tendons, his head thrown back, and a roar of pleasure echoed in the otherwise silent room.

I don't know how long we stayed like that, panting, trying to drag in another breath. My body was still quivering, Liam continued to thrust shallowly inside me, and I struggled to keep myself upright.

"You make me lose my mind, baby. Every time I think we've managed to satisfy each other, I find myself wanting you again," Liam admitted behind me.

"I know what you mean," I answered honestly. Liam kissed my shoulder, my neck, and then slowly pulled out from me.
I sat back on shaky legs and turned to look at him. His dark blue eyes were serious again, and he cupped my face.

"Why do you make me this crazy?" he asked. He wasn't looking for an answer though; I knew he was asking himself more than me. I leaned in and kissed him softly before I stood back up.

"We should get going," I reminded. Liam nodded and stood, and I watched as he readjusted himself. I excused myself to go to the bathroom and spent a little time cleaning myself up. I slid on a new set of underwear, applied a little makeup, put my hair up into a fancy twisted ponytail, and I was ready. When I entered the room, Liam stood up and smiled, his gaze sweeping over me.

"Beautiful, as always," he commented. I inwardly sighed and looked up at him.

No one was perfect, not even Liam. But damn, the man came close.

CHAPTER TWELVE

"Mel… is that carpet burn on your knees?" Max asked an hour later as we sat in a booth at the bar, pointing to the red marks. I felt my face flame up immediately and looked at Liam. The guys started laughing, and I laughed too.

"I'm betting Liam has a matching pair on his knees," Seb added. Liam reached over and slapped his friend up the back of the head, but they both chuckled.

"Is that why you two were late?" Kade asked with that Scottish lilt to his words, a knowing glint in his pale eyes.

"What the hell were you doing looking at her legs, anyway?" Liam asked, glaring at Max.

Max held up his hands as if in surrender, and I smiled at his attempt at innocence.

"So, what are you going to do when you get back home, Mel? What's waiting there?" Max asked. An awkward silence settled over the table, and I flicked a quick look at Liam and then away.

"Not a lot. My job is waiting, but since I've never taken a holiday, they were more than happy with me taking time off. Bree, my best friend, is there. You guys would love her," I assured them. And then we got to talking about the many exploits of Bree and the trouble she'd gotten me into and out of over the years. By the end, everyone was laughing harder than ever.

"You'll have to bring her here for a visit sometime," Max suggested. I nodded, glancing at Liam again and then away. Maybe I would.

"I gotta hit the head. Be right back," Seb announced.

"Another round?" Max asked. We all nodded, and Kade went with him to get the drinks. The music changed, and I stared in surprise at Liam's hand suddenly in front of me.

"Dance with me?" he asked. I smiled and let him pull me up from the booth. We walked hand in hand to the dance floor, and I smiled when Liam spun me around and then up against him. One of his hands kept hold of mine, and the other rested on my lower back as he moved us around. It wasn't a slow song, but it was a song that let us stay close together.

"So…" Liam began, and I smiled against his chest.

"So," I repeated.

"Tomorrow is the big day."

"Yep," I answered, feeling myself tense up.

"What time is your flight again?"

"I leave at six a.m.," I answered. Liam nodded against me, and I waited, holding my breath.

"Mel... do you think..." he started, and I felt my heart pound harder in my chest.

Would he?

I pulled back to look up at him. His blue eyes considered me seriously, nervously.

"Uh, will you let me drive you tomorrow?" he asked.

I tried not to let disappointment sink in or show on my face. I plastered on a smile and nodded.

"That would be nice, thank you," I answered softly. My voice was a little scratchy, and my eyes stung, so before I gave away that I was tempted to cry I leaned my forehead against his chest and swallowed hard, closing my eyes. I knew this was how it was going to go, so I was not going to cry and ruin this.

We danced around for the following two songs, and when I was sure I would not cry, I even managed to laugh a little and enjoy myself. Liam was too easy to be around and so much fun. "My turn. Can I cut in?" Sebastian called. We turned to see Seb standing beside us with his hand out.

"I'll go get another drink," Liam said when I smiled. I nodded and laughed when Sebastian spun in and made me twirl him under my arm. Seb was fun too and very easy to talk to.

"So, I've been wondering about something," Seb said conversationally.

"What's that?"

"Are you going to tell Liam you're in love with him? Or are you going to leave and never come back?"

I stiffened and looked up at him in complete and utter shock. "W-what?"

"You heard me." He smirked. "And don't bother denying it. We can all see it, clear as day. You don't want to go any more than he wants you to go."

"And you'd know this, how?" I asked, finally regaining the use of my mouth. "Mel… I've known the guy for a few years now. And I've never seen him act with a woman or look at a woman the way he does with you. You're special to him, and from what we can see, the feeling is mutual."

I didn't answer, too busy wishing and hoping what he said about Liam was true. I wanted to be special to him; I wanted to be someone different than the other women who had spent time with him. I wanted to be more to him than they were.

"If Liam really felt that way, he would have asked me to stay rather than asking if he can drop me off at the airport," I refuted softly.

Seb grinned and shook his head, spinning us around a little. "When you're faced with what you want more than anything else, and what you want can walk, talk, and think for herself *and* hide her emotions, it's hard to put yourself out there and reach for it."

I considered what he said, but my heart was too shy to accept what he was saying. "Yeah, I get it."

It was exactly how I felt.

Seb smiled knowingly at me but thankfully let the subject drop. We danced a little longer, and I laughed when Sebastian forced me into a position to dip him. He was definitely a clown.

Hours later, I was beginning to fall asleep on my feet, but I didn't want to call it a night because if I did that it meant I was that much closer to going home, and my time with Liam would be over. I know, it was kind of pathetic and desperate, but I liked who I was with him; I enjoyed being with him and spending time with him. Just the way he smiled lit up my day, and I loved watching the emotions run across his face and the way his eyes seemed to change with feeling. I didn't want to say goodbye to all of this.

"Mel, you're almost asleep," Liam told me, tugging on my hand.

"No, I'm not," I denied and then gave a yawn so big my jaw ached. Liam chuckled and tugged me against him, and I buried my face against his chest.

"Come on, babe. Let's say goodnight," he suggested softly. I nodded. As much as I wanted to stay out, I could barely keep my eyes open.

We stopped to say goodbye to the guys, and I took a moment to hug each of them and thank them for making me feel so welcome. And before I knew it, Liam and I were outside his house again. The wind was a little more intense tonight, and I stood there for a moment with my eyes closed, dragging the sea air into my lungs.

I didn't have to open my eyes to know Liam was standing in front of me. He had an air to him, something intangible but noticeable. I slowly opened my eyes and looked up into his aqua gaze, his eyes searching. I wanted to ask him if he wanted me to stay, ask him if he wanted me like I wanted him. I tried to tell him how I felt about him—the words were right there on the tip of my tongue. But when I tried to ask, my throat closed over, and the words died in my mouth.

Maybe it was for the best. Perhaps this was all we were ever meant to be. Maybe, this small window of time together was something we both needed to move onto the following chapters of our lives.

Liam took my hands in his and walked backward slowly until we were inside his house. He closed the door, and I looked up into his shadowed face and sighed. "Let's go to bed, Mel," he whispered. I nodded, and he leaned forward to kiss me. It was slow, exploratory, gentle. His hands were soft on my waist as he pulled me forward, and I felt myself melt against him.
On and on, the kiss seemed to go, deepening and turning into something more. It was as if we were trying to say all the things we needed to say without words. Tonight was goodbye; we both knew it. But neither of us said it; neither of us wanted to acknowledge the enormous truth that this was probably it for us. Our journey ended here.

Tomorrow, things were going to be different.

But we had tonight.

~

I glanced back at Liam on the bed, the sheet barely covering his lower half, the rest of him bare. He had one arm curved up over his head, and the other rested gently on his chiseled stomach. His hair was dry now, and some of it curled lightly over his forehead. I clenched my jacket around me as I took a moment to soak in the image of him, sleeping and unguarded.

I couldn't say goodbye, not to him. No, that wasn't right. I couldn't say goodbye and not have him ask me to stay.

Actually, there was one other scenario that would be worse than either of those. If I said goodbye, told Liam how I felt, and then he had to let me down easy. I couldn't take it, couldn't handle the rejection and the heartache. Instead, I was going to take my memories of him as he was now, as he had been throughout this entire week, and hold them close. I was going to take these memories, untarnished and unbroken.

After kissing me like I was the last woman alive, the heat had turned up significantly and we'd stumbled further into the room and hadn't even made it to the bedroom before we were naked and on each other. Liam had me pressed over the back of the sofa that first time. Not long after, we'd had something to drink and gone back to bed, but he hadn't stopped touching me, stroking me.

Soon enough, we were intertwined again. For the rest of the night, things had been slow and intense. He'd kept his eyes locked with mine as he thrust inside my body, his expressive gaze trying to tell me whatever he couldn't or wouldn't say out loud. I hoped he understood what I wanted to say to him. I wanted him to know how I felt, how much it was tearing me apart to leave. But he still hadn't asked me to stay, hadn't asked me not to go. He hadn't even so much as hinted at it.

So, we spent the night touching, kissing, and watching each other fall apart over and over again. Sometime around two in the morning, we'd shuffled into the shower and washed each other before falling into bed together.

I'd laid in his arms, listening to Liam breathe and fall asleep. I could have fallen asleep, but I knew it wasn't a good idea for him to wake up with me in the morning. Honestly, I'd been thinking about it since he'd asked to drop me off at the airport. Which was why I'd used my time in the bathroom at the bar to call the car service and request them to pick me up from the house two doors down from Liam's place and take me back to the hotel. I had to collect my things and then head to the airport, and I didn't want him to take me. I couldn't face saying goodbye, and I didn't want to have to get on that plane and watch him *not* ask me to stay.

Liam shifted in his sleep, and my heart clenched.

I looked once more at the dresser where I'd left him a note and straightened up.

It was time to go.

I silently picked up my shoes and the overnight bag I'd ended up bringing here, and with one last look at him asleep on the bed, I left the house. My heart was breaking, but I refused to acknowledge it, refused to feel it. I had to get on a flight in two and a half hours. I had to make it through a ten-hour flight, convince Bree that I was fine, and then once I was back in my apartment I could fall apart.

The ache in my heart intensified and threatened to break me, but I sucked in a deep breath and pushed aside my emotions. I had a plan in place, and I would work through every phase. I wasn't allowed to break down until I was safely ensconced in my apartment at home with the door locked, a mountain of chocolate and vodka.

The car service took me back to the hotel and I looked around the room I hadn't even slept in. Everything was immaculate. Not wanting to hang around pointlessly, I packed up what was there of my things and made my way downstairs to the lobby. The car service booked for the airport was early, so before I knew it, I was on my way to the airport and back to reality.

~

I'd been waiting at the airport for what felt like forever I'd had two cups of coffee, nervously eaten a donut, and was flicking through my phone, looking at all the photos of Liam and me over the last week.

You're mine, Mel. Mine.

I'm yours, Liam, just yours.

Those words kept going round and round in my head. The way he'd said them, the pure ownership and command in his eyes and on his face. The possessive way in which he held me to him. Was that all a lie? Had I misread it all, and he was just playing a part for a week?

How pathetic was it that in the back of my mind, some idealistic part of me still hoped I'd see Liam come running through the airport looking for me? That my heart actually believed he'd wake up without me, see my note, and come running and ask me to stay?

Pretty pathetic, huh?

I jumped slightly when a woman on the PA announced my gate was now boarding. Swallowing back the regret, I got reluctantly to my feet. I looked around me one last time and then shook my head at myself. It was time to go; time to get on the plane and put it all behind me.

CHAPTER THIRTEEN

Three days.

Three long, *miserable* days.

Bree had picked me up from the airport, and as soon as we were in her car and she wrapped her arms around me, I broke down in tears. I wish I could say that I hadn't cried on the plane, but unfortunately, my seatmate got an earful of my tragic heartbreak. She was nice, though. She gave me tissues, she listened, and offered advice where she could. I would have been embarrassed, but I was just too damn tired to care.

Bree was a good friend. She let me cry the whole way home, and then she walked me upstairs, where she already had ice cream stocked in my freezer—coffee, my favorite—and my favorite comfy pajamas ready. I dressed and then sat on the couch with my ice cream and best friend while watching *The Princess Bride*.

After a few hours of watching me sit in misery, I'd insisted that Bree go home so that I could really ugly-cry and act in a way that would be embarrassing in front of my best friend. I promised to call her in the morning, and she left. I spent the night watching

The Princess Bride on repeat, eating my coffee ice cream, and crying over my Vacation Journal.

Day two involved a lot less crying, but I was still moping around my apartment and had no intention of showering or answering my phone or door. I called Bree as promised but warned her that I was hibernating for a while and to not bother calling. I knew she was worried, but I didn't want to talk to anyone.

On day three, I finally unpacked my suitcase from my vacation, put away the journal, and cleaned up my apartment. I called Bree, who insisted on meeting her for dinner that night—just the two of us so I wouldn't have to watch how perfect she and Jay were. I told her not to do that, she and Jay were permanent, and I didn't expect her to change the way things were to make me feel better, but she insisted.

So, I showered and shaved and got dressed up. I still felt like crap, but I knew it was time to pick myself up and get moving on. Besides, I had work again in a few days, so it was time to get on with my life.

My phone rang as I was heading out the door, and I stopped to answer it when I saw it was Bree.

"Hey, what's up? I'm just leaving," I answered.

"Oh good, I caught you. I'm running late. I won't be home for about another hour if you can wait. Sorry, I got caught up at… work," she answered.

I frowned at her excuse. "You mean you and Jay had a quickie at his office, and it's going to take you that long to get presentable and get back home?" I corrected.

She laughed, and I shook my head and grinned.

"Okay, you got me. Just wait, I'll let you know when I'm home, and then you can leave. It'll give me time for a shower before you get here," she answered.

I sighed. "Okay, I'll be waiting," I agreed, even though a part of me saw this as a reason not to bother leaving the apartment tonight. I could hear my couch and comfy pajamas calling to me.

I frowned when there was a knock at my door. No one came over here, no one but Bree. And I knew she was on her way to her apartment. I looked through the peephole and frowned when I saw no one. Cautiously, I opened the door and gasped.

A huge vase of red roses sat in front of me, glorious and full of color. I gaped and then looked down the hall for a sign of anyone, but no one was there. Carefully, I picked up the vase, astounded at the weight of it, and put it on my kitchen counter. I looked through the flowers for a card and smiled when I saw one. With trembling hands, I opened it, and my breath caught at what I read.

If it takes every 80's movie grand gesture to win your heart, then...

As you wish...

~ L

This couldn't be... no. These weren't from... Liam? Another knock at the door. I hurried over to it, kicking my foot on the edge of the couch as I moved, which slowed me down, but no one was there when I opened the door.

Just a diary.

I picked it up and saw the following note.

To record the new adventures that I hope we'll share together.

My heart was thundering now, and I took another look down the hallway, but there was no sign of anyone. How was he doing this? Because it had to be Liam, he was the only one I'd ever told about the whole romantic gesture thing.

Music blared from outside, and I closed my door and hurried to my window, a giggle trying to escape my throat. Outside I could see an actual boom-box sitting on top of a car, and I gave a choked laugh even as tears filled my eyes at the sound of *Say Anything* blasting from its speakers.

My phone rang and I slid away from the window to answer it.

"Hello?"

"Unlock your window for your fire escape."

"Bree?" I frowned.

"Just do it!" she squealed excitedly.

Before I could even move, there was a slow, deliberate knock from the window at my fire-escape.

Licking my dry lips, I hesitantly turned to look. The music had stopped now, and as I got closer, I could see him there.

Liam.

He was on the landing outside my window with his hands shoved into his jean's pockets, his familiar aqua eyes locked on me.

He was real. He was here.

I paused at the window, seeing the vulnerability there and the nerves. Sucking in a deep breath and wiping at the tears on my cheeks, I lifted my window and climbed out onto the fire escape. Liam backed up so that I had room, and I smiled tremulously up at him. "Hey, you," he greeted softly in that way he always did, his deep voice sending a shiver up my body. Yeah, I hadn't imagined how he affected me.

"Hi," I breathed, and my voice broke.

He studied me carefully, and the silence between us grew steadily. "So, it turns out if you go running through an airport— even a small one—without a boarding pass, you *will* get arrested by airport security."

I froze as the implications of what he was saying sunk in, and then I laughed. He smiled, looking a little relieved. "You ran through an airport?" I asked, trying desperately not to cry or reach out and touch him.

He was here!

"I did," he answered with a slow nod, those dark eyes serious. I watched as he pulled out his phone, and he showed me a photo, and a watery laugh escaped my lips. It was a photo of him with two airport security men holding a sign saying, *"Sorry we stopped him, Mel!"*

He put the phone away, and he sighed and looked down at me.

"I woke up in bed three days ago, hoping to pull my woman in close and beg her to stay with me," he began in a low voice.

I swallowed hard, and he stepped forward, stalking me. "You did?" I whispered, edging back slightly at the intensity of his gaze.

He nodded and kept edging closer. "I had this entire speech prepared, how I was going to tell her what she means to me, how much better my life is with her in it. I was going to try and use my body to persuade her if that was what it took. I was prepared to have my heart crushed on the off chance that she didn't return my feelings," he explained, and my heart clenched painfully, and butterflies took flight in my stomach.

"But then I rolled over, and she wasn't there. I think I knew she was gone right away, but I checked the bathroom too and looked at my phone, but there was no message. I turned to see a note on my dresser," Liam explained, digging the paper out of his pocket. "A note which told me she had enjoyed her vacation, that she had loved seeing me again, and that she hoped we could stay in touch," he continued, the displeasure, hurt, and confusion clear in his voice.

"Oh, and there was a little postscript," he added, his eyes still clinging to mine as if he were searching for an answer for something. I swallowed and nodded, knowing what I'd written, knowing that I'd felt foolish and as though I was leaping from a cliff, leaving those words there.

"She added on the bottom that she'd fallen in love with me five years ago. And that seeing me again had made her realize that she'd never stopped."

He shuffled closer, and I felt my back hit the stone wall behind me, my heart pounding hard.

"Imagine how happy I was to see those words and how furious I was to find her gone. Imagine my frustration when I ran from my house and through the airport, dodging security to try and make it to her gate in time, only to find myself detained and forbidden to go after her."

I shivered at the heat in his eyes, at the swirl of emotions that he was barely keeping in check.

"So, after an hour of explaining what I was doing, and after calling in a favor so that I would not be arrested by the police or fined, I made my way back home to think of a plan. Obviously, I'd failed my first attempt at an epic declaration of love that running through an airport at the last minute would have displayed," he continued

I choked on a laugh, and before I could wipe away the tear on my cheek, his hand was there. His thumb ran back and forth over my cheek, and he stared at me with some overwhelming emotion.

"You told me that your version of how a relationship should start should be something like an eighties movie. Now, we didn't exactly start that way, but then again, we both expected it to be temporary. But just like you," he started and dragged in a steadying breath. "I fell in love with you five years ago, and I've hated myself ever since for walking away. I thought I was doing the right thing, bowing out, letting you and my friend be happy together. I stayed away once, and that was a mistake. I'm not about to make the same mistake twice."

My heart was soaring, and my head felt light, but I refused to believe, refused to breathe, until he said the words I needed so desperately to hear.

"Mel... I ran through an airport for you, and we both know how that turned out. I don't know how to draw like Leo, so I can't draw you like he did for Kate. I saw you writing incessantly in that journal of yours, so I decided to follow Colin Firth's lead and buy you a new one for you to fill with new stories and adventures like he did with Bridget, because I never want to stop giving you those," Liam told me, and I felt myself smile and a small laugh escape at the fact that he was naming some of the best romantic couples of all time, even if they weren't all eighties movies.

"If it takes building your dream house like Noah did for Allie, then I'll do it. I would have bought you a thousand yellow daisies like Max did Lorelai in *Gilmore Girls*, but you love red roses, and…well… those fuckers are expensive."

Another small laugh slipped out even as another tear tracked down my face that he'd remembered the details of our conversation where I listed a crazy amount of romantic gestures in movies and T.V. shows.

"I'd take a bullet for you like Costner did in *The Bodyguard*, but I'd prefer to avoid that one if I can. I will do all of this and more. Hell, I'll strive to get you the library from *Beauty and the Beast*. Whatever you need for you to see that I want *you*, Melanie. I fell in love with you five years ago, and the feeling has only intensified in this week we spent together. Please tell me I'm not too late."

It took a moment for me to be able to speak without blubbering.

"I came home intending to get over you," I started, and I watched as his blue eyes swam with turmoil. "But just like I told you on the island, you will always be the exception for the things I have planned for myself. Of course it's not too late, Liam. It's never too late for you."

My voice broke towards the end of my sentence, and Liam's smile lit his entire face. He didn't allow me to speak another word before he swooped down and kissed me. I gripped his arms and kissed him back, feeling the tears on my cheeks but unable to do anything about it. It had been hell the last few days thinking I'd missed my shot at love—because that's what this was.

I could hear clapping and whooping, and we pulled apart to see Jay and Bree on the level below us on the fire escape. Jay had his arms wrapped around Bree while she jumped up and down, pumping her fist into the air.

"Would you two please knock it off? And get off my fire escape!" Mrs. Wendel from the floor down reprimanded.

"Hey, we're here watching a moment of true love. Stop hating life long enough to let the rest of us enjoy this moment, you old bat," Bree snapped back.

"Sorry ma'am, we're leaving," Jay apologized and started helping my unruly best friend down the stairs.

"But I want to stay and talk to Mel," Bree complained.

"I'm fairly certain Mel is going to be otherwise occupied for some time. You can call her tomorrow," Jay assured her as they reached the bottom. Bree pouted, but Jay silenced whatever complaint she had by picking her up and kissing her senseless.

I laughed shakily, and Liam grinned and turned back to me.

"I love you, Melanie Gellar," he whispered.

"I love you, Liam Mathews. Thank you for not giving up on me."

"Never," he murmured before kissing me again, his tongue brushing against mine and his body pinning mine to the wall.

God, I'd missed him, missed this.

No one kissed like Liam; I was sure of it.

EPILOGUE

Six months later, I sat on a stool at the Salty Bar & Grill, smiling at the band as they rehearsed for tonight's set.

Liam and I had spent a crazy weekend together after the night he came to get me. We didn't leave my apartment, and besides one call to Bree to update her, we didn't talk to anyone. It was one of the best weekends of my life.

Not long after, we had a discussion about what to do. Long-distance didn't work for either of us, and when it came down to it, I would have been crazy to choose the city over an island paradise.

So, I'd handed in my notice, and two months later I was living on L'Amour Island with the love of my life. Bree was a little upset about the distance, but she understood and was happy I'd found someone who made me so happy and who treated me so well. She and Jay promised to visit often, and I would see her in the city when I could. Turns out, Liam had been drowning in paperwork with the bar and hated that side of things, so I took a job managing the finances and dealing with order forms and trying to book in local talent a few nights a week. I was incredibly excited about my new job.

"Alright guys, I think we're all set for tonight," Liam said to the band. They all nodded in agreement and set their instruments aside.

"Hey, Mel, here's the new menus we had done at work," Anna called as she entered the Bar. I turned to see the beautiful red-headed woman approach with a pamphlet in her hands. I'd entered into an agreement with the owner of one of the island's restaurants that we'd hand out cards with discounts on them for tourists in the bar, if he'd put an advertisement for our bar on his new menus. While we did cater some food, it wasn't restaurant quality, and we were one of the only places with live music, so it was a win-win.

"Oh, great. Thanks, Anna. How's work?" I asked.

She smiled kindly and nodded. "You know, same old. Nothing too new. How's it going with Liam?" she asked with a wink. I couldn't have stopped the grin on my face to save my life.

Anna laughed and nodded to the menu. "So, what do you think?"

I perused the menu and smiled down at the promotional picture. It had a photo of the bar with all the boys in one corner of it, displaying that we had live music most nights. "I love it; it looks great."

"I thought so too," she answered. I looked back up at her, but her eyes were trained on something behind me. I spun slightly on the stool so that I could see what had caught her attention, only to see Sebastian standing at the base of the stage, flirting with some woman.

Sighing, I shook my head. "Are you and he ever going to sort out whatever went wrong between you?"

Anna shook her head and sighed. "Probably not," she replied with a shrug.

I frowned. "Will you tell me what happened?"

She smiled, but it was forced, and her eyes were sad. "Maybe someday."

Just then, Seb looked over at us, and his eyes locked on Anna. "Gotta go," she said quickly and spun on her heel to march out of the bar.

"Anna!" Seb called out and chased after her. I shook my head and smiled as Liam approached me.

"Hey, you," he greeted and leaned down to kiss me quickly. My heart still fluttered at the sight of that smile and the look in his eyes.

"Hi," I answered as he leaned close to me, caging me in against the bar.

"What did you think?" he asked.

"The band sounded great. I gotta say, the lead vocal is hot, though. I would have tossed my panties at him if I could," I answered.

Liam smiled and leaned closer. "Why didn't you? The guys would have been jealous."

"Oh, it's not that. I'm just not wearing any," I whispered against his lips.

Liam froze, a breath away from kissing me, his dark eyes flickering with arousal. "Are you telling the truth?" he asked, his voice low and growly.

A shiver snaked down my spine, and my breasts felt suddenly achy.

"You'll have to find out for yourself," I teased.

Liam made a slight growl low in his throat and liquid heat pooled low. "Come with me."

"Or what, sir?" I teased further.

"Or you'll be punished," he threatened.

A thrill ran through me; his punishments were always something I enjoyed. "Where are we going?"

"My office," he answered darkly.

"And what will we do there?" I asked facetiously as he tugged me towards the hall.

He turned dark, heated eyes on me, and I grinned. "We're going to find out if you are lying about your panties."

"I'm a good girl; I never lie," I teased as we reached the door. Liam groaned and pushed through the door, spinning me around the second we were inside and shoving me against it. His mouth came down on mine, hard and intense, his hands running down my hips as he slowly bunched my skirt in his hands and raised it further up. I tested his strength, tried to pull away, but he shoved me back again, slamming my arms back on either side of my head.

"Don't. Move," Liam ground out. I nodded, excitement and arousal running through me, and he slid his hands up my thighs to my bare pussy and groaned as he slid his fingers through my slick folds.

"Fuck," he groaned.

"See?" I panted.

Liam kissed me again, intense and quick as he unzipped his pants and shoved them down. Almost immediately after, he grabbed my hips, and I helped him as he wrapped my legs around his waist. Quickly, Liam adjusted us, and I was impaled on his thick, hard length. Our moans intermingled, and Liam thrust hard; once, twice, and then he was fully inside me. I gasped and looked at him, constantly overwhelmed by the way I felt when we came together.

"I love you," I breathed unevenly. Liam stilled, and I watched him swallow hard before he kissed me gently. I frowned at the sudden change in his demeanor, and he smiled.

"Marry me."

I gaped, my eyes widening. "What?"

"Marry me," he repeated, thrusting inside me. I cried out and held on tightly.

"Liam… we haven't even been together that long," I reminded, moaning again as he thrust inside me over and over.

"We've loved each other for over five years. Marry me, Mel. I know this is right."

I cried out, and when I didn't reply, he stopped and ran his fingers through my hair, turning my face to look at him. "I love you more than anything. You make my life whole. I'm not the same without you. Marry me, Mel, be my wife."

"You're serious?" I gasped.

"I have a ring at home in the drawer. I've wanted to ask since I brought you back here. I mean it, marry me," he said again.

I rocked against him, unable to stop myself, and he made a sound of pleasure. I watched his face, the love burning brightly for me, the heat, the passion, and the need. We fought sometimes; we were both passionate and not afraid to tell the other when we thought each other was wrong, but we loved just as passionately and more often too. I knew that I wanted no one else. He was it for me. Why not start now?

"Yes," I whispered. Liam's eyes widened, and he stilled.

"Yes?" he repeated.

I nodded and smiled, a small laugh escaping. "Yes, I'll marry you."

Liam leaned forward to kiss me happily, and then he was moving again, in and out, short, hard thrusts that left me panting and begging.

"Liam," I pleaded.

"Let go, baby; I've got you. I'll always catch you," he panted. Far sooner than I would have thought was possible, my climax hit me, and stars burst behind my eyes. I cried out his name and ground against him, my eyes closed as pleasure took me over. Liam soon followed, his body shaking hard against me as he came inside me, his thighs trembling.

"I love you, Mel," Liam whispered again.

"I love you, Liam," I answered, and we met in the middle for a long, leisurely kiss.

I never once would have believed that my Vacation Hook-up would have resulted in me falling in love. And not just that, but having a second chance with the man I had let go so many years ago.

Maybe this really was the island of love...

THANK YOU FOR READING!

ABOUT THE AUTHOR

DID YOU KNOW…
I HAVE TWO OTHER PEN NAMES?

I know that seems like overkill, but there is a method to my madness.

Books under the name **Alexis Maree** are for paranormal romances. Not everyone likes to read this genre, so I like to keep them separate.

Likewise, not everyone likes contemporary romances, so I have another pen name for those…**T. Maree**.

Then last, but certainly not least, are my sinfully sexy romances, the ones that border on the line of "*should she really put that down in print?*"
Some people don't like those kinds of spicy scenes, and so I decided to keep those separate from the rest under the name **Luna Maree**.

So, if you'd like to check out what else I've written, go onto my website

Happy reading!

Alexis | Luna | T.